A MOULDY DESTINY

Visiting Guyana's Forbes Burnham

James W. Ramsahoye

MINERVA PRESS

WASHINGTON LONDON MONTREUX

A MOULDY DESTINY
VISITING GUYANA'S FORBES BURNHAM
Copyright © James W. Ramsahoye 1996

All Rights Reserved

ISBN   1   86106 130   7

First Published 1996 by
MINERVA PRESS
195 Knightsbridge
London SW7 1RE

2nd Impression 1997
3rd Impression 1997

Printed in Great Britain by
B.W.D. Ltd, Northolt, Middlesex

A MOULDY DESTINY

Visiting Guyana's
Forbes Burnham

About The Author

James William Ramsahoye is one of five brothers and two sisters born to Jairad and Wilhelmina. All of the children were born and grew up in Guyana. They all received their higher education in Europe, America and the West Indies and have rendered distinguished service to their country in science, engineering, medicine, law, business and sport. His father, Edward Jairad Ramsahoye, attended the Queen's College of what was then British Guiana in the early years of this century.

James, who was born in 1936, also attended Queen's College, like his father before him and three of his brothers. He later entered Canada where he took his Bachelor of Science degree in Microbiology in 1965 at the University of Alberta in Edmonton. He continued his studies there and took his Master of Science degree in Food Science in 1967 and his Master's degree in Business Administration in 1970 majoring in Organization and Marketing. He worked as Director of Procurement and Distribution at the Misericordia Hospital in Edmonton before joining the Marketing Division of the Guyana Bauxite Company in 1972. He was its first overseas representative for North and South America and Asia from 1973 until 1987 when he was appointed overseas representative for Europe.

He has taken great interest in the historical development of British Guiana and has studied the country's economic and social decline despite its enormous resources and human talent since it became independent in 1966. His book, *A Mouldy Destiny – Visiting Guyana's Forbes Burnham*, is his first published work and accurately reflects Guyana's condition in nearly one third of a century since independence. At its core are references to the political promises and deception which have characterised the development of and performance by Guyana's political directorate under L.S.F. Burnham. Since then political power has been used and abused to the detriment of two generations of children of his country. Throughout his work the first phase of the country's plight under inept leadership after independence is clearly revealed. There will be more for him to consider about the ensuing period which followed the demise of Burnham and the assumption of his powers first by H.D. Hoyte and later C.B. Jagan.

It remains apt for him to say that Guyana is bathed in tears. There is tragedy but no triumph. There is a spoils system which is inherently oppressive. Education has declined. The quality of the environment is impoverished. The nation is in a desperate search for political ability and political morality which are necessary prerequisites for the cessation of its decline and a resumption of its progress. Ramsahoye is a patriot who writes out of loyalty to his country and sympathy for his countrymen who since independence have borne the severities of deprivation and exile at the hands of its ruling political class. He must remember John of Gaunt and knows that Guyana never could lie at the foot of a political conqueror until it first makes a shameful conquest of itself. He must know too that the people of Guyana see in the words of the Scottish chieftain immortalised by Tacitus that its rulers are capable of destroying its institutions and creating an economic and social wilderness even as they promise prosperity and peace.

Introduction

The PNC believes that there should always be free elections, freedom of speech, freedom of worship and other freedoms and, much more important, freedom from hunger and the freedom to work. Those were the words of the now deceased Linden Forbes Sampson Burnham spoken on 27th March 1961 in a radio broadcast to the Guianese people prior to the general election of that same year. Four years later, after taking over the reins of power and becoming Prime Minister, in a report to the nation on 12th July, 1965, he said, *It is my conviction that Guiana as part of the Caribbean has a contribution to make to the world, a tale to tell – the tale of how a small nation can act independently without making itself a participant in the Cold War – a tale of how a small nation can evolve a way of life of its own – a tale of how a small nation can, with the energies of its people and the assistance of real friends, banish poverty, plan its economy and maintain democracy. This contribution we cannot make, this tale we cannot tell, unless we have full independence.* British Guiana became independent on 26th May, 1966. Let history and those who write about history comment on the events and experiences of Guyana under the maladministration of the dictator and the People's National Congress (*PNC*) after those words of comfort.

This book is not about the biography of Forbes Burnham, nor is it a history of his tenure in Government. It is about observations made from reading his speeches contained in his book published in 1970 and titled *A Destiny To Mould*. The speeches in the book contrast very much with the behaviour of

Burnham after his ascent to power in Guyana. Whereas hope and great expectations were offered in the speeches, in reality Guyana's experience during his tenure as head of the country for almost twenty-one years was a terrifying exposure to ruthless dictatorship. Under his stewardship, all of the institutions were destroyed and accountability to the people was erased. Burnham's lifelong ambitions, which he achieved, were political power and domination. He was never a conciliatory leader and used his cunning to great advantage over the opposition.

Illegality, corruption, incompetence, nepotism, inefficiency, discrimination, mismanagement, repression and tyranny were rampant. The once loyal police force and the army became tools of the PNC, the political party that he headed, and together with the People's Militia, the National Service and 'Rabbi' (David Hill – a fugitive from America) Washington's gang were used to keep the people subdued. On 29th September, 1963, in a speech at a Special Congress of the PNC he said, ...*if a people are determined to stand up against dictatorship, if they are prepared to stand up against an attempt to rob them of their freedom in any field, it is very unlikely that the would-be dictator can succeed.* The backing of the forces mentioned disproved that. An atmosphere of fear entrapped the Guyanese people and although Burnham did not use the same mechanisms as Adolf Hitler through mass destruction, the methods applied extracted the vital spirits of those who were targeted. There was no physical exertion of pain on the many who were considered to be not in unison with the PNC and the 'Flounder Leader', but when he was finished you were totally discombobulated and devastated. Complaints could never be corroborated by broken souls. The world could not see destruction of the spirit. Adolf Hitler's methods were crude but visible and were recorded for all posterity. Many Guyanese fled from Burnham's reign. Families and individuals are now scattered and dispersed, like windborne seeds, across the globe.

As I read through the honey-coated speeches I could not help but think that the actual happenings were as changed as when pleasant wine turns to vinegar. The speeches are model speeches if action did not follow but the eventually destroyed state of Guyana demonstrated that the words were full of sounds and echoes emanating from a large and empty vase. Their contents are proof that the man was an impostor since they conflicted with his deeds. The people of Guyana lived through a nightmare until 6th August of 1985, after which it retracted to being a very bad dream. In a short space of time a country, which was considered the one with the most potential for success in development in the Caribbean, found itself grappling for its existence and becoming a pauperised state. Power and absolute power at that was the basic root cause but complementing the destruction were the various experiments in political governance and the several attempts at reinventing the wheel. There was the belief that the country had to be totally destroyed before it could be rebuilt. The country was considered as Plasticine which could be squashed and reshaped. The human content was irrelevant. The people became the toys which Burnham lacked in his youth. He played with their lives as the Romans played with the lives of the Christians and slaves. He must have been a bitter youth experiencing an awful childhood.

A driving force entered my mind after reading the book and I found myself wanting to record how chameleon in character Burnham the 'Flounder Leader' was using his book to achieve my aims. I told myself that I could not allow the book to stand alone without bringing to light the inconsistencies of the book as evidenced by acts that followed. During the time when Burnham was alive there was hardly ever the opportunity to criticise or speak out against his undertakings. I was not brave and I, in all humbleness, did not consider myself a David who was about to defeat Goliath! Better sense prevailed. A better man had tried it and now he is just a memory having reached oblivion's gates. My efforts are not meant to speak ill of the dead but to see that posterity is not robbed of the actions of Guyana's first and hopefully last dictator. It was Burnham, when addressing a mass crowd at the Parade Ground in Georgetown on 18th November 1962 after the collapse of the 1962 Constitutional Conference and making reference to Dr Cheddi Jagan, who said, *I do not want to be hypercritical. They say: 'of the dead speak no ill'; I would say: 'of the weak, speak no ill'*. For me, it is: 'of a tyrant, write what you know and how you feel'.

Burnham took advantage of the Guyanese people because he was given the gift of eloquence above all other Guyanese. No one in the country could deliver a speech like he could, and he was truly set apart, and this ability to speak as if it were music afforded him the opportunity to mesmerise those who followed and believed in him. But, just as Fate could be gracious with the gift of speech Fate could also bestow a curse. For Burnham the curse lay in the organizations that he touched by nationalisation and the development projects he planned. All failed. Unlike Midas who had the golden touch, Burnham was endowed with the faecal touch. Bauxite, sugar, rice, Nigerian palm oil, hydropower, the glass factory, the cooperatives, the External Trade Bureau, the educational and health systems, the public utilities, the judiciary, the Civil Service, the police, the army, and almost everything else failed in their respective ways. Only the Demerara River Bridge and the Linden Highway escaped, symbolic of the fact that they were the only acts of unity since the bridge linked the banks of the Demerara River and the road gave easy access to Mackenzie, formerly accessible only by river or air, now renamed Linden and which was about sixty-five miles directly south of Georgetown. It never was like that when he first came to power but as he started to develop the illegal mechanisms for retaining power and entrenching himself forever, Destiny, never forgetful, counteracted with matching failures. Was it because he did not have the legal right to be in charge since all of his electoral victories from 1968 onwards were counterfeit? I do not know, but the evidence is there to be seen on the faces of the Guyanese people who have been battered and degraded, similar to the physical state of the country.

Sic fatur lacrimans (bathed in tears), I recall growing up in the garden city of Georgetown. It was so beautiful and clean. The houses were beautifully painted as well as the fences, the streets were smoothly paved without potholes, the gutters were clean as well as the parapets, the canals were not clogged and most important of all there were no mosquitoes. Our potable water system was one of the best in the world. There was adequate and reasonable public transportation. All of that changed during the Burnham years. The once beautiful city became – 'ugly town'. I remembered Guyana as a place of great hospitality as evidenced by the courteous and kind treatment offered by friends on visiting. That too changed as living conditions deteriorated and that warm hospitality could not be extended anymore because of the difficult circumstances. And I will always remember Guyanese Christmases because there is no other place in this world that can express the tidings of joy at the birth of Christ like Guyana. Even with the deprivations Christmas in Guyana was unmatched. And do you know that the dictator made heavy efforts to de-emphasise Christmas in Guyana and suggested that it be replaced with Mashramani, a type of carnival? The happiest time of the calendar year for the people was to be minimised. Fortunately, because of their strong religious convictions and their hopes that they were not forsaken, his aspirations could not take root. This was the man who, after being put into power, in a radio broadcast to the nation on Christmas Day, 1964, said, *Happy Christmas and may God bless you all brother Guianese – my friends, my people*. Absolute power now gave him the right to tell the people to forget Christmas thus attempting to destroy their spiritual faith.

In this book I encounter Burnham in the Underworld in a forechamber where men of evil have to spend an unlimited time receiving punishment for their criminal acts. It is a purgatory similar to that experienced by Guyana but more punishing. The encounter is really a monologue as Burnham is unable to speak having lost that ability in the Upperworld. He is represented by the speeches in his book which remains for all to read but accept with a grain of salt. In mythology others had gone to visit the Underworld for some reason or other and they were successful in reaching there and returning back to the Upperworld.

My sincere hope is that readers may find solace in knowing that the only book published by Burnham does not stand without a response in the libraries of the world. For if it did, as it has been doing so far, then posterity would have looked unkindly to those who have witnessed the systematic destruction of a small and beautiful country and allowed the passage of time to pass without comment. I am no Simon Weisenthal, but it is necessary to bring to light the evil which surrounded Guyana in a period of its history. We are now in a period of history where disclosure is assuming a greater importance. It is an avenue that must be used to the full in an effort to guide us in the future and to stave off potential onslaught. I hope that others who are more knowledgeable would be courageous enough to come forward and record in depth a detailed history of Burnham's administration.

One of the first stories I was exposed to at school was 'Belling the Cat'. I have done so and others may now proceed in safety.

When a man knowingly commits wrong, he is
wrong and furthermore it must be acknowledged
that he has committed a wrong.

This book is dedicated to all of those Guyanese, living or dead, abroad or at home, who have had to suffer in one way or another under the regime of Forbes Burnham and his accomplices; and to the children of Guyana who must have the courage to ensure that another era of gloom and darkness never visits Guyana again.

*"Creep, walk, run, jump, hide,
The truth has no refuge to abide."*

GUYANA

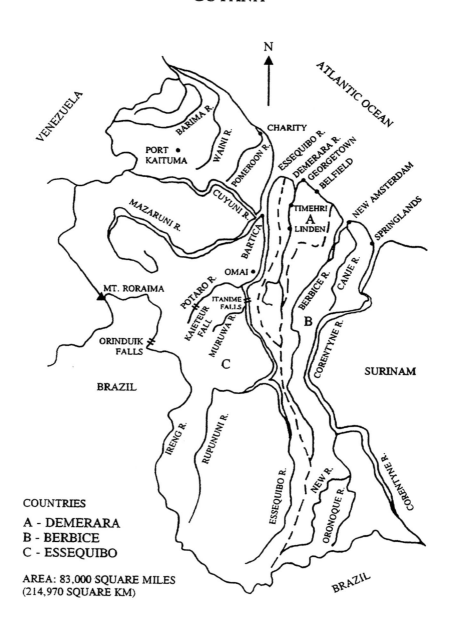

N

ATLANTIC OCEAN

VENEZUELA

BARIMA R.

WAINI R.

PORT KAITUMA

POMEROON R.

CHARITY

ESSEQUIBO R.

DEMERARA R.

GEORGETOWN

BELFIELD

NEW AMSTERDAM

SPRINGLANDS

CUYUNI R.

MAZARUNI R.

BARTICA

TIMEHRI

A

LINDEN

OMAI

BERBICE R.

CANJE R.

MT. RORAIMA

POTARO R.

ITANIME FALLS

KAIETEUR FALL

MURUWA R.

B

CORENTYNE R.

ORINDUIK FALLS

C

SURINAM

BRAZIL

IRENG R.

RUPUNUNI R.

ESSEQUIBO R.

NEW R.

ORONOQUE R.

CORENTYNE R.

COUNTRIES

A - DEMERARA
B - BERBICE
C - ESSEQUIBO

AREA: 83,000 SQUARE MILES
(214,970 SQUARE KM)

BRAZIL

Chapter One

The Queen's College or QC as it was nationally known started out as Queen's College Grammar School on 5th August, 1844, and was founded by The Most Rev. William Percy Austin, D.D., who was at the time Bishop of British Guiana. Its first formal school building was located at Carmichael and Murray Streets in Georgetown. Murray Street has been renamed Quamina Street. This building was occupied in 1854. In 1876 the school was renamed The Queen's College and the student body numbered over seventy as compared to fifteen in 1844. In 1918 the school moved to Vlissengen Road and Brickdam where it remained for thirty-three years until it moved to its present site at Thomas lands in September 1951 at Thomas and Camp Roads. The student body was well over five hundred by this time. The school was considered the best of secondary schools in Guyana, maintaining that position to this day. It was one of the foremost in the British Caribbean territories, if not the foremost.

Sunday July 31st, 1994, heralded the commencement of six days of activities commemorating the 150th anniversary celebrations of the founding of The Queen's College of Guyana. QC advanced through those 150 years from that wonderful day of August 5th, 1844. Since that time it developed a reputation for being a secondary school of excellence in the arts and sciences. To this day it is still, without competition, the leading school in Guyana despite enduring serious neglect. The school, always known for its academic performance, blossomed from its commencement and its fruits sprouted forth becoming prolific after the end of the Second World War. Students of learning having left there entered the world of adulthood equipped to assume all the responsibilities that were to confront them in the years ahead.

I wended my way to the Queen's College site at Thomas Lands accompanied by my younger brother Walter. On our way to the building we had to traverse streets inundated with potholes and it necessitated a high degree of manoeuvring to ensure that the car did not find itself anchored in one of the holes. My immediate reaction to the vehicle's weaving in and out was that had the captain of the oil tanker *Exxon Valdez* been exposed to a lesson in manoeuvring similar to this then the unfortunate accident which occurred at sea off the coast of Alaska in 1989 would have been avoided. The state of the roads was symbolic of the decay that had taken hold of Georgetown, once regarded as a garden city. Buildings were shabby and needed painting and this once beautiful city was in a derelict state despite thirty-two years of peace and tranquillity. It was sad to have to traverse such an uninspiring environment. Georgetown, the capital, was once so beautiful and sparkling. Now it seemed as if a complete overhauling was required to rehabilitate this capital of a country which I remembered as being as large as Britain. When I left in 1960 to pursue studies abroad the population was close to nine hundred thousand. Today, the population stands somewhere between six to seven hundred thousand. Political change gave impetus to the exodus, not only of people in general but also some of its most professional stalwarts. Almost every scholar of integrity was forced into exile. In retrospect it was quite obvious that they saw the writing on the wall. They were the visionaries. The sad part about the emigration was the splitting up and separation of families. The pillars of human civilization crumbled. Here was another application of the divide and rule principle.

Having parked the car on Camp Street we proceeded east to the building. I had first set foot on this pathway forty-three years before when the building was opened for regular classes in 1951. It was a spectacular wooden building and I was very proud to have had the opportunity to attend classes there. The building was huge as compared to the old school in Brickdam where I started and it catered for a student population that was much larger than those attending in the Brickdam building. In 1975 the school became coeducational and presently there are 359 female students. Prior to this girls were strictly students of science and came to QC to take classes in Physics and Chemistry for the London Advanced Level examinations. To the south of the walkway and the building itself could be seen houses for accommodation by the Principal and Senior Masters. These buildings now appear in need of repairs and painting. They had joined the queue of derelict buildings that demanded attention. It was a shameful sight.

I entered the building and proceeded by way of steps to the auditorium. I was handed a programme. On entering the auditorium the first thing that I noticed was that the light was subdued because portions of the northern side of the auditorium were boarded up. The auditorium was also not as cool as it used to be. The school was less than seven hundred yards from the Atlantic Ocean and thus was subject to the prevailing trade winds. These trade winds with their gentle breeze kept the auditorium cool. Subsequent enquiry indicated that there was need for extra space to accommodate additional rooms for teaching, hence the boarding up of the northern section. At this stage I thought that an apology was due to the architects of the building, for in their wisdom they had seen the need not only for light but for a cool environment since more than one thousand people would be assembled in the auditorium on many occasions. Their wisdom had been intruded upon.

No sooner had I walked a few feet on the time-worn floors when I started to greet other alumni. It was so good to see the gathering of the clan and to observe the many faces of those who had returned from far-off lands to celebrate this auspicious occasion. Immediately, I met a fellow alumnus whom I had not seen for forty-five years. He was now a doctor in the United States.

Although he was very senior having been in the sixth form when I started out at Queen's, I recognised him for in his day he was an athlete of renowned speed. I first met him at the old school in Brickdam. There were others there whom I met overseas and I now saw them again for the first time since. It was a wonderful occasion and the Alma Mater must have been proud to see alumni gracing the auditorium to celebrate the sesquicentennial anniversary. It was only thirteen years before its founding that the counties of Essequibo, Demerara and Berbice were united to form the colony of British Guiana. Thus the School could be considered as old as the colony. It was an occasion for celebration and of sweet nostalgia. Memories of this place were all full of joy and happiness.

In the auditorium there were several rows of chairs separated by a wide passage which ran east to west. On the stage were chairs for school officials, honoured alumni, guests and alumni who would deliver addresses on behalf of the various chapters of the School Alumni Associations abroad. I sat on the southern side of the auditorium looking east and facing the stage. Looking down on me were the Honour Boards which had registered on them the names of all of those who had won the Guyana Scholarship as students of Queen's. I was very proud to see the family name appearing twice – 1949 and 1960. The two names were those of two of my three brothers who attended Queen's. Five of us were therefore forever in gratitude to the school since my father was also an alumnus.

It had provided us with a sound education and upbringing. The names on the board did not say that the two names which were the first and second respectively, had won a scholarship with three distinctions each in science in the history of the school. Both brothers achieved the same feat of gaining distinctions in Pure and Applied Mathematics, Physics and Chemistry. Proud I was but not without some envy. In the field of the arts, the first person to gain distinctions in Latin, French and Spanish was in 1958. Sources reveal that in 1960 the scholars were so brilliant that students from Queen's had won all six scholarships offered by the University of the West Indies, but only three were awarded to Guyanese as it was not deemed politically correct to have one country being awarded all six.

It was shortly after ten o'clock when the proceedings commenced with the singing of the national anthem followed by a hymn. The principal, Mrs D Rutherford, the first woman to hold such an office in the school's history, delivered the opening and introductory remarks. Thereafter, several speakers addressed the gathering. All spoke of the excellence of the school, its long history and of its deteriorated state. No one mentioned the architect of its demise. The singing of the school song *Laude Gratemur Scholae*, in existence since 1919, brought the opening ceremonies to a close. Afterwards, attendees were invited to a Creole brunch in the dining hall adjacent to the south of the auditorium. A series of athletic activities and a cricket game were planned for the afternoon session of the celebrations but, unfortunately, the weather was inclement and those activities had to be postponed.

On Monday August 1st, there was the opening of an exhibition, mainly of photographs giving a historical perspective of the school. It was also the occasion of the launching of the book *Queen's College of Guyana – Records of a Tradition of Excellence (1844-1994)* written by alumnus Dr Laurence Clarke. The book was well-received and contains a wealth of information about the school since its inception. A family Fun Day was spoilt by inclement weather once more. I took the opportunity at this session to sign up with a party to tour the Kaieteur and Orinduik Falls in the interior the following day.

On Tuesday August 2nd, I received a telephone call telling me that the trip to Kaieteur was postponed and would now take place the following day. This gave me an opportunity to attend a Symposium on the 'Role of Queen's College in the 21st Century'. Once more there were several speakers and also audience participation. The excellence of the school was reiterated and discussion centred on what could be done to restore the school to its former glory. It was quite evident that there was a degree of scepticism about the future of the school. Apart from a dire need of funds to do repairs there was a need to find a formula which would attract qualified teachers. The meeting ended with no consensus but suggestions were to be put to the authorities.

In the evening there was a cocktail party hosted by the President of Guyana, Dr Cheddi Jagan, an alumnus of the school and leader of the People's Progressive Party (PPP). The event was held on the lawns of the President's residence and was well-attended. Fortunately, rain did not interrupt the festivities at all.

On Wednesday August 3rd, after a lengthy delay, the touring party set off for the Kaieteur and Orinduik Falls. The Kaieteur Falls is situated on the Potaro River, a branch of the Essequibo River, in the heart of Guyana. It is magnificent and a sight to behold. I had visited Kaieteur twice before. The first time was in 1959 when I worked in the Agriculture Department on a field trip engaged in looking for soils suitable to grow cocoa. The second occasion was in 1976 as a tourist. Whilst travelling in the aircraft on the way to the falls I could not help but think of the forest's canopy which reminded me of a bunch of broccoli. The forest was very thick and this broccolic vision stretched for miles and miles. Below that canopy lying dormant was part of Guyana's wealth. Kaieteur Falls was in all its splendour as the dry season did not have its full effect at which time its grandeur is diminished. It was breathtaking! There is no doubt that this could be a major tourist attraction of Guyana and it is a sight for all the world to see. Proper development and supervision would ensure its success as a tourist attraction.

After leaving Kaieteur the party headed for Orinduik Falls situated further inland in Guyana and to the south-west of the Kaieteur Falls on the Ireng River. The Orinduik Falls in contrast to the Kaieteur, which has a perpendicular drop of 741 feet, is step-like and is nowhere as high. Visitors often take the opportunity to have a wade in the water there as I did. It is a beautiful set of falls but not as majestic as Kaieteur. This was my second visit to Orinduik, the first time being 1976.

Returning from Kaieteur I attended a Caribbean Jump-Up at Queen's on the lawns. The music was that of the Caribbean. It was well-attended to the point where I would say it was crowded. I had an enjoyable time and took the opportunity to chat with alumni and friends whom I had not seen for quite a while. Despite some lengthy discussions about the school and its deteriorated condition no one mentioned the name of the person responsible for placing the school in that diminished position.

On Thursday August 4th, I did not attend any activities at the school. However, in the evening I attended a piano recital given by alumnus Hugh Sam at the National Cultural Centre. It was a splendid evening of musical entertainment, and Hugh, as usual, was the master of the keyboard. He played his composition based on the school song *Laude Gratemur Scholae* for the first time, which included quotations from other melodies. I remembered Hugh's playing when he attended QC and he always enthralled us with his piano choices of Chopin, Mozart, Schumann, Liszt, Schubert and other great composers.

Friday August 5th, was the last day of celebrations and there was to be a general assembly in the morning followed by a formal dinner and dance in the evening. During the week, I meandered down memory lane on many occasions and could not forget how fortunate I really was to have had the opportunity to attend this school. There were moments of deep sadness observing its present state. Starting out with fifteen students in 1844 it reached a maximum of eight hundred and twenty-two in 1985. The school now catered for seven hundred and sixty-three students. I understand that another secondary school called the President's College was established, hence the decrease in student population. The establishment of the President's College was targeted to diminish the stature of Queen's. Accelerated deterioration of the School seems to have started thereafter. I was disturbed at this thought and was filled with disgust at the thought that a school which had established itself in the British Commonwealth had been subject to whims which would eventually lead to its degradation.

Fortunately, this was no ordinary school and it had established itself as the leading school in the English-speaking Caribbean, earning at the same time respect from the authorities of universities in far-off lands. The school was regarded as a centre of scholarship and excellence and with its transition to a co-educational facility it now offered equal opportunities for boys and girls. It had served the educational needs of Guyana in the past and was prepared to continue that service. Its reputation as an institution of learning and for providing a good education bolstered it and many Guyanese parents still wanted their sons and daughters to attend Queen's. They recognised that when a student would look back after leaving the school their memory would remind them what a remarkable and exciting experience they had had and how lucky they were to be part of its alumnus. The school had been the fountain of knowledge for students of varying social and ethnic backgrounds and its aim at all times was that each individual should be able to reach their full potential. It encouraged activities, academic and non-academic.

I arrived at the school's auditorium shortly before the commencement of ceremonies. Attending the ceremonies and giving the feature address would be the President of Guyana. I took a seat once more below the Honour Boards. Prior to sitting I collected some papers from a friend, having asked him to bring them for me. I myself had a brown envelope. I could not help but think how those very boards were bound with the memories and sentiments of generations of QC students. The boards could boast of a glorious past and hopefully they were looking forward to a matching future. Looking around me I could not resist thinking that the school was at the heart of Guyanese leadership. It had produced so many prominent figures not only for the nation but for other countries which welcomed emigrating alumni and their families.

I was listening to the chairman's remarks and thinking that the greatest threat to the school's survival was not the physical deterioration but the need for qualified staff and continuous funding to keep that staff. My mind was not at ease as I was still outraged at the architect of the school's predicament. Ingratitude, ignorance, and lack of understanding of how greatness develops were at the foundation of its floundering state. I was fuming inside when suddenly I was startled by a strange feeling and then I heard a soft, spooky voice.

Chapter Two

"Fourth son of Jai and Wellie, be not alarmed! You are unhappy and disturbed throughout these celebrations as a heavy thought weighs upon your mind. I know that thought. There have been many speakers and speeches and no one has been bold enough to name the architect of the deterioration of the school. No one has had the courage to speak out aloud. This Alma Mater of yours you hold so dearly; it has moulded so many of greatness and fame. Your unending sadness and pain are so intense that I have been sent to give assistance in comforting you.

"Hear me oh troubled one! For you will be given an opportunity to address the one who occupies your mind. You have been chosen because of your travels in the Upperworld. You are one of the most travelled alumni of this school, if not the most, but your belief in this school sets you way beyond many others. You have defended this school at all times and you have only spoken words of praise. You have held the view that had it not been for the actions of the one who disturbs your mind that the works of the school's alumni would have lifted this country to a height of envy. Today, your fellow alumni abound elsewhere and make their contributions in lands afar. Their exodus was forced upon them and so they went away, but in their deepest thoughts the golden time of their days at this school surfaces. Son of Jai and Wellie, you have announced that you have had the opportunity to live in paradise and that you would not exchange nor trade your time between 1936 and 1960. I recall when you left this land for another in 1960 to take up further studies. You who have travelled to great cities of the world in all directions will not budge from your belief that you did walk in the land known as paradise, known as British Guiana at the time. Whenever you think of that time you can only recall happiness and joy."

As I listened I wondered how it was possible for the voice to know who I was thinking of since the person in my mind was long dead. The voice had indicated that I would come face to face with the one who was troubling my mind. To achieve that I would have to visit the land of the dead. How did she know that I was thinking of Forbes Burnham who died almost to the date nine years before? I wanted to meet Linden Forbes Sampson Burnham, first President of the Cooperative Republic of Guyana. I knew he was in the Underworld but in which section was unknown to me. Beckoned by this spiritual voice my wish was to be granted.

Forbes Burnham was born on 20th February, 1923, in the county of Demerara, in the Colony of British Guiana. He was of humble parentage. He was very bright at school in his junior years and this attribute helped him to gain an outstanding education at The Queen's College of British Guiana from where he won the British Guiana Government Scholarship in 1942 after obtaining distinctions in English and Latin at the Higher School Certificate examinations of the University of London. In 1945 he proceeded to London University where he gained an Honours degree in Law. Whilst at London University Burnham won the Best Speaker's Cup of the Faculty of Law. He qualified as a barrister in 1948 from Gray's Inn. It was said that he was a student of Marxism.

In 1949, Burnham returned to British Guiana and soon after started on his political career by teaming up with Dr Cheddi Jagan and becoming a founder member of the People's Progressive Party (PPP). In the general election held on 27th April, 1953, the PPP were triumphant in winning eighteen out of the twenty-four seats that were contested. Dr Jagan became the Premier and Forbes Burnham the Minister of Education. In

October of that same year the Constitution was suspended and the PPP were removed from office following reports from the British representatives in British Guiana that the PPP was setting up a communist state. An interim government was installed.

In 1955, during party affairs, a split occurred in the executive branch of the PPP, and Burnham left the PPP to form his own faction. Retaining the name of PPP, his party was known as the Burnhamite Faction of the PPP. Likewise Jagan's party was called the Jaganite Faction of the PPP. Both men wanted to use the name PPP since it had gained enormous popularity and it was the beacon party. This splitting of two powerful personalities gave birth to the racial division in politics which exists to this day. Black Guyanese followed Burnham and East Indians followed Jagan. The fabric of the country's make-up was almost completely torn apart. What was achieved in 1953 was put asunder. British Guiana would never be the same again!

Elections in British Guiana were fought under the system of first past the post as prevailed in the United Kingdom. The country was divided into a number of constituencies. After a period of Interim Government from 1953 to 1957 new elections were called in 1957 and the constituencies were reduced from twenty-four as it was in 1953 to fourteen. The Jaganite Faction of the PPP won the election by winning nine seats. The Burnhamite faction won three seats. Soon after this defeat Burnham decided to rename his party and called it the People's National Congress (PNC).

The fourteen seats Parliament continued in operation until 1961 when new elections were held with expanded constituencies. Parliament was to have thirty-five seats, an increase of eleven and twenty-one respectively over the 1953 and 1957 elections. In that election the PPP won twenty seats and the PNC won eleven. The PPP had gained 93,000 votes and the PNC 89,000 votes. These results fuelled the calls of the PNC for a change in the system of election. They advanced a system of proportional representation as a replacement for the age-old first past the post system. The air that blew on the fire to make it hotter was Communism. Burnham had found that under the multiconstituency system there was no way in which he would be elected to government outright. He wanted to be in power. This was his burning ambition. This was his goal. Whatever had to be done to achieve success in that end was embarked upon. During this period of government the PPP administration was plagued with riots and disturbances with the PNC in the forefront. It was a period in history that many Guianese would like to forget.

The British Government wanted to grant independence to British Guiana but Burnham kept plugging away at the discrepancy between votes gained and seats allocated. He pressed for a change of the electoral system, campaigning relentlessly towards that end and urging that proportional representation be implemented. The British were in a dilemma since there had to be a justification for changing the system since they themselves were ruled by the system of first past the post. Numerous conferences and meetings were held to decide what was to be done in British Guiana's case.

Across the Atlantic in the United States the word Communism had taken on the appearance of Medusa's head. It was feared and dreaded, and as British Guiana was located in their hemisphere, and it was well-known that Dr Jagan was a Marxist-Leninist, they wanted an end put to the progress of the PPP. Many in the State Department knew that Burnham was an opportunist and a demagogue but when compared to the Communist Jagan he was the lesser of the two evils. It was pointed out that the best chance to remove Jagan democratically was to impose the method of election by proportional representation. There probably would not be an outright winner and thus an accommodation would be in the offing. The viewpoint of the United States influenced the British Government and it was finally decided that the electoral system in British Guiana would be changed from first past the post to proportional representation. The PNC was overjoyed.

In December, 1964, the first election under the new system of proportional representation was held and Parliament would now be composed of fifty-three members. Under this system the country was to be one constituency and seats were to be allocated on the basis of votes received by the contesting parties. At the end of the counting of votes the PPP were allocated twenty-four seats, the PNC were granted twenty-two and a third party, the United Force (UF), headed by Mr Peter d'Aguiar was allocated seven seats. Despite the PPP winning the majority of seats Dr Jagan was not invited to form the government. This was contrary to convention and it was quite obvious that the objective was to see that he was kept out of government. The new government was formed by a coalition of the PNC and the UF with Forbes Burnham becoming Premier and Peter d'Aguiar the Minister of Finance. Dr Jagan became the leader of the Opposition. The PNC was regarded as a Socialist party, its leader being grounded in the teachings of Karl Marx. The UF was labelled pro-business and capitalist. Mr d'Aguiar may have been pressured to team up with Burnham and because of his support he cannot go blameless for Guyana's predicament since he afforded an opportunity to Burnham, thus setting him on his journey to destroy Guyana. The coalition was a marriage which found two strange bedfellows cohabiting. Needless to say it would never last and divorce proceedings were not long in being filed.

Burnham, in the meantime, whittled away at the Opposition to gain a majority in government by getting Opposition members to cross the floor and join his party, knowing that such a move was illegal since members who occupied seats in Parliament were nominated by the party. Under proportional representation it was the party which put up the candidates. The crossover exercise undermined the very principle of constitutional government, destroying at the same time representative government, since those who were nominated on the party's ticket were no longer representing the voters who had voted for the nominating party. The discarding of the system of first past the post removed the power of an individual candidate to join the party of his choice should there have been a change of heart. Achieving this change of partners was the first indication of how serious Burnham was bent on being in full control. The defections ensured the fertilisation of the sterile egg which laid dormant guarding the dastardly plans which Burnham held in his mind. The plans that could not be seen. The matured zygote freed its devious plans and their implementation became the poison that would alter and destroy the people and their aged and veritable institutions. Those spineless sperm defectors contributed very substantially to the destruction, irreparable harm, loss and damage that Guyana suffered. Without them Burnham could not install the mechanisms which would enslave the Guyanese people as he would not have had a majority in Parliament. The fear of Communism played its part for when wrongs were being committed financial support still kept flowing and was as constant as the flow of the Essequibo River into the great Atlantic Ocean. That financial support was given to ensure the huge public debt in the knowledge that the country would never be in a position to repay and thus be subject to pressure from its creditors. This pressure became vividly clear when the Guyana dollar on instructions from the International Monetary Fund (IMF) was devalued from $10G for $1US to $33G for $1US in 1989 finally settling in 1991 at $125G to $1US. In 1970 the exchange was $2G for $1US. Cuffy, the national hero, is probably turning in his grave to know that slavery has returned. He was not knowledgeable about modern political and economic slavery. The works of William Wilberforce and Rev. John Smith became fruitless as the Guyanese were now enslaved not by force but by economic factors. A new form of bondage developed from which there was no easy escape.

Constitutional talks were held with the British Government and British Guiana was granted its independence on 26th May,

1966. The talks were attended by the PNC and UF only as the PPP decided to boycott those discussions. I have always felt that it was not the best decision of Dr Jagan. It was well known and accepted that certain powers did not want Dr Jagan to be in power but he was the representative of close to fifty per cent of the people of British Guiana and therefore his contribution would have been weighty. He would not have been the leader but whatever he wanted to be enshrined in the constitution of Guyana would probably have been implemented. The situation was similar to a car having passengers but Dr Jagan was not the driver. He was still a passenger and had every right to safeguard the journey to his destination. He was in the front seat and had access to the steering wheel.

Forbes Burnham took over power in British Guiana in 1964 and remained in that position seeing the country through to independence in 1966. In 1967, d'Aguiar resigned from the Government as Minister of Finance and the marriage between the PNC and UF was granted a decree absolute with Forbes Burnham as the presiding judge. Burnham now being in total control of the election machinery strengthened his hold on an independent Guyana through electoral fraud beginning with the election of 1968 and those that followed in 1973 and 1978. He introduced for the first time overseas voting placing on the overseas electoral lists names of persons dead and alive and whose residences were fields and pastures. The country under his domination became a republic in 1970. Thereafter, he upgraded himself from Prime Minister to become an executive President of the Cooperative Republic of Guyana. During his tenure of office the country moved from one of great promise to one which found itself at the foot of the world's economic ladder. Burnham turned to dictatorship and authoritarianism unleashing a reign of fear and suppression. Continued success with counterfeit victories bestowed upon him indisputable power. Institutions of government were brought into disrepute and the physical state of the country was decrepit. Mass emigration took place and Guyanese sought refuge in any quarter that would accept them. The promises that he had made in his quest for power were those typical of politicians who feel that they must anaesthetise the public in order to win their confidence. Burnham's unequalled oratory was used to administer the local anaesthetic. The danger there of course is what happens after the anaesthetic has worn off and the patient afterwards is no better off and in all truth worse. Such was Guyana's fate as Burnham failed to perform. A strong infant country was not allowed to be developed despite the fact that of all the British colonies to gain independence British Guiana was perhaps the one which had the most promise since it had abundant natural resources and a highly literate and articulate population though small. It could have been a saviour to neighbouring Caribbean States not only as a producer of food, goods and services but as a repository for immigrants seeking a better homeland. His death on August 6th, 1985, apart from bringing freedom from tyranny, ended an era during which Guyana instead of becoming economically independent found itself thrown back into the dark ages through electoral fraud, destruction of its institutions, and the breaking of the people's spirits through fear and suppression. In the wake of all his destructions Burnham had included in his repertoire The Queen's College of Guyana. I had not paid a visit to Queen's for about twenty years prior to my attendance at the sesquicentennial celebrations and therefore when I saw what had happened since that time I became infuriated. I could not allow history to pass without commenting on Burnham's role in the demise of the school and the destruction of Guyana. I had always spoken of his evil doings but now I could no longer be constrained and it was time that the written word was recorded. The message of the voice though frightening made me feel glad as an opportunity was being presented to me.

After hearing the pronouncement of the voice, immediately I felt scared and I remembered how scared I was one night when I was returning home after seeing two horror movies at the Empire Cinema in Middle Street. It was 1950 and I was about fourteen years old and I distinctly remembered that one of the movies was *The Mummy's Curse*. It was close to midnight when the show ended. I had gone with some friends who lived nearby in First Street. I lived at Lamaha and Albert Streets and had to walk about two and a half blocks alone to reach home. As I turned from Light Street into Lamaha Street crossing the road to walk on the pavement on the northern side of Lamaha Street I thought I heard footsteps behind me. I hurried my steps and soon it was only half a block to home. I lived on the second floor of the building and there was a long stairway leading from street level to the top of the stairs. At about one hundred yards from the bottom of the stairway I looked up to the top of the stairs and I thought I saw a figure dressed in white. Shivers went up my spine. The mummy had passed me unnoticed and was waiting for me. How one's imagination can run away? In my present situation I felt scared at the thought of encountering anything that was not alive.

Recalling that incident brought back memories of the railway which ran parallel to Lamaha Street and which carried eastward those beautiful engines. I remembered *Sir Graeme, Sir John, Sir Edward*, all big engines, and also the smaller engines: *Donkey, No.8* and *No.3*. Such wonderful memories! Now there is no railway in Guyana despite it having laid claim to being the first country in South America to have a railway. That claim was lodged in 1847. The removal of the railway signalled the future misfortunes of the country. When there are not many good roads and traffic is heavy rail is the best way to move freight unless there are waterways to do the job.

"Do not be afraid. You will not meet with any mummy in this place that I will take you. You will be visiting the front halls of the Underworld. My time with you is limited and, therefore, I must send you on your way. Concentrate and you will find yourself travelling fast and distant as if heading for the bowels of the earth. You will eventually come face to face with the one you seek. You will be able to address him but he will not be able to speak to you for do not forget he has lost the ability to speak. Therefore, I caution you that whatever you say must adhere to the truth and be honest speculation as he cannot reply in his defence. Remember that this subject is in the forechamber, one of many to the final resting place. His initial ordeal has to last an unlimited time since apart from his crimes he has attempted to cheat Death. I say this because his symbolic body and that of another rest, not in the places reserved for the dead but in the place of the living – the Botanical Gardens, which as you know is home to the zoo, the manatees, those lovely birds and those beautiful trees and flowering plants. It is a place where since its inception people have gone to relax and enjoy the pleasant surroundings. It is a place for lovers and is not suitable to accommodate the dead. It harbours life and should do so forever. Therefore, until such time as their bodies are removed their time in the forechamber would be endless. In the Upperworld there are places reserved for the acceptance of the dead body. These normally are the cemeteries, the sea, the compounds of the Church and the crematorium. There are occasions when one of those places cannot be reached and special dispensation is given but once it is possible to reach one of the named places, then it is imperative that the body takes its occupancy in one of the designated places. No place other than those mentioned is normally ever used to hold the dead body.

"The one you seek will find rest in three of the named places. The exception is the compound of the Church for history records that there were efforts on his part to de-emphasise celebrations in Guyana in honour of the birth of the Child of Bethlehem. It was an effort on his part to destroy the spiritual faith of the people. He sought to undermine the very reason for their being. Therefore, his symbolic body cannot abide in the sacred ground of the Church. The body of the second person will be accepted in any of the four named places. Until such time when those bodies are removed from the land of the living their souls shall endure endless discomfort. Their presence in the land of the living also casts a curse upon the rest of the land and thus their removal is most urgent and must be accomplished.

The forechamber I speak of is also reserved for those who have committed the gravest crimes against mankind in some form or manner. It is not a place of happiness and, therefore, be not surprised at the agonies you see. Many of the souls that dwell there were once leaders and had the opportunities to do deeds of exaltation and praise but their egoism made them do otherwise. The environment of the forechamber is not pleasant, it being a place where punishment must be endured – the air is foul and the temperature hot. Creatures proliferate and insects fly incessantly and numerous monsters abide in this wretched place. Yet, be not afraid for you will not feel any of the discomforts. You will be under my protection at all times and you will be comfortable throughout your visit."

As the voice spoke, my thoughts were travelling back in time and I remembered starting out at Queen's in September of 1948. Prior to that I had attended Bedford Methodist School in Georgetown which was situated opposite to Bourda Market in Robb Street, and opposite Bedford on the diagonal was a huge open park now occupied by a host of market stalls. I saw myself walking from Church and Light Streets where I lived, having moved to Georgetown from Plantation Hope on the East Coast in 1945, to Queen's in Brickdam adjacent to Vlissengen Road. I saw myself dressed in a white shirt, khaki pants, 'A House' tie (red, yellow and black) and my safari-type helmet (bug house/cork hat). Along the way I had to pass the home of Deputy-Principal Mr H.A.M. Beckles at the corner of Light Street and North Road on the eastern side, Frolic Hall at the north-west of Light and Robb Streets, and which in this same building at street level was housed Mr Dalzell's parlour (snack shop), the Polar Bear Rum Shop at Regent and Light Streets in the south-west, and Susamachar Church at the corner of South Road and Light Street on my left. I can say that Mr Dalzell was one of the first marketing innovators in Guyana as he gave free of charge butterscotch candy based on the quantity of bread and cakes that were bought.

I remembered my class 2A being housed in the main building on the bottom floor and in the western corner. It was all coming back and the memories were pouring in like torrential rain. Queen's in Brickdam was home to scholars and the male educational elite of British Guiana at the time. To be afforded an opportunity to attend Queen's was a giant leap in the hierarchy of life. I considered myself fortunate and Bedford Methodist faded away although it would never be forgotten. I had graduated from primary to the secondary level. Having entered Queen's I knew I would always be proud of having graced its doorsteps, classrooms and playing fields. My future was assured.

The three-storeyed wooden building in Brickdam was flanked on the east and west by two playing fields respectively. The western field being about six times as large as the eastern. Connecting the main building to a southern building was a covered corridor and this corridor was always a known place of assembly during breaks. The tuck shop was housed in the southern building. The joy of having a lemonade and a bun there still surfaces. East of the south building was found the home of the janitor Mr Green, known to the boys of the School as 'Drone' since his reaction to stimuli was very slow. Beyond the south building was Hadfield Street. It was in this Queen's College of Brickdam that I was exposed to Latin and where I read of mythological Orpheus visiting the Underworld to retrieve his beloved Eurydice and also of the visit by Trojan Aeneas to the same place to converse with his departed father Anchises as told in Book VI of Virgil's epic, *The Aeneid*.

Orpheus visited the Underworld to retrieve his young bride Eurydice who died after being bitten by a snake. They had not been married long. He charmed the rulers of the Underworld Pluto and Proserpine with his music and they agreed to let Eurydice return to the Upperworld on the one condition that Orpheus was not to look back until he reached the upper air.

Orpheus agreed but in his anxiety seconds before he reached the top he turned to get a glimpse of Eurydice only to see her receding back to the place whence she had come. Further efforts on his part failed and he died of a broken heart. In Aeneas' case he visited the Underworld to speak with his father who disclosed to him his future destiny as the founder of the Roman nation. Aeneas returned safely to the Upperworld after his visit.

Vivid in my memory as a member of 2A was my first game of cricket in the Third Eleven. It was played on the eastern field which separated the Geography classroom from Vlissengen Road. We won the game outright and thus gained three points. I recalled F.E.M. the captain of the first eleven congratulating us on our victory. I later found out that the championship of cricket in the School was awarded to the house with the most accumulative points from the First, Second and Third Eleven competitions. 'A House' or Percival House unfortunately, did not win the 1948-1949 competition. 'C (Austin) House' did. Recalling those events took a fraction of a minute.

Yet as the voice made its delivery I was hearing the presentation from the podium. Prior to this assembly and at another time during the celebrations other speakers had spoken of the school and of its history and of its fame for producing scholars. Some spoke of the present derelict state of the building and how there was need to make a concentrated effort to bring the school back to its former times. This was easy to say, but hard to achieve. It reminded me of those famous Latin words from Virgil's *Aeneid*, book VI, *Facilis descensus Averno, sed recovare gradum superasque, hic labor, hic opus est!* Translated, 'Easy is the descent to Hell, but to retrace one's steps to the Upperworld, this is toil, this is work!' It was not just a question of the physical state of the building that had to be remedied but grappling with the greater problem of the teaching staff. Matters had deteriorated to such an extent that there were not adequate qualified teachers. The low wages being paid could not attract qualified teachers. This was a grave problem and had to be confronted and resolved. The quoted Latin words were not only applicable to the school but were also aptly suited to the state of the country. It too had descended into Hell. Destroyed it was and to put it back into some workable state would call for a tremendous input of money, discipline and hard work. The legacy left made all of these requirements difficult to achieve. The destruction and waste of both Queen's and the country lay at the hands of a former alumnus. How ironic that a school reputed for fame and greatness could also harbour a wrecker of property, institutions, lives, hopes and dreams. This was the thought that bothered me that no one had the testicular apparatus to say that it was a Queen's boy who was responsible for the miserable state of the school, that it would require another Queen's boy to rehabilitate it and perhaps also another Queen's boy to keep it maintained as an institution of greatness. Rejuvenation, maintenance and death all came from this institution as if the sweet, the bland and the bitter can never be separated.

"Hear me, Chosen Traveller! The forechamber is of vast expanse and harbours souls of all those who have committed some unforgivable acts. In the case of your objective let me tell you he placed himself above the law of the land, and of the people.

"He countenanced himself as being as powerful as the Almighty. Even his son-in-law was nicknamed Baby Jesus. It is well-known that a service of thanksgiving was held at Westminster Abbey on 9th October, 1985, for him but even that could not help him evade this place. He was of the view that no punishment would ever be meted out to him. Let me tell you that only the pure and good-hearted can escape punishment. Punishment in the Underworld varies according to the misdeeds committed. It varies from a tiny penalty to relentless affliction.

"You are aware of an article of the present constitution of Guyana wherein the President is immune and cannot be faced with civil nor criminal charges whether in office or not. In other words he is immune from punishment and therefore as President he is endowed with power usually held by the Unseen. Article 182 (1) of the constitution states: *Subject to the provisions of article 180, the holder of the office of President shall not be personally answerable to any court for the performance of the functions of his office or for any act done in the performance of those functions and no proceeding, whether criminal or civil, shall be instituted against him in his personal capacity in respect thereof either during his term of office or thereafter.* It continues in Article 182 (2): *Whilst any person holds or performs the functions of the President no criminal proceedings shall be instituted or continued against him in respect of anything done or omitted to be done by him in his private capacity and no civil proceedings shall be instituted or continued in respect of which relief is claimed against him for anything done or omitted to be done in his private capacity.* Finally, Article 182 (3) states: *Where provision is made by law limiting the time within which proceedings of any description may be brought against any person, the period during which any person holds or performs the functions of the office of President shall not be taken into account in calculating any period of time prescribed by that law for bringing any such proceedings as are mentioned in paragraph (2) against him.*[a]

"Thus, no law is applicable to the incumbent of such an office. However, down in the forechamber there are no such laws, written or otherwise, and every person who enters those quarters, and everyone must enter at some time or other, has to undergo some form of punishment. There are no courts as you know it but judgement is passed upon the individual based on completed acts of guilt and those acts are known to the individual and so once committed they are registered in the book of life.

---

[a] *The Constitution of the Cooperative Republic of Guyana 1980.*

"The one you seek was of the view that no punishment would have been meted out against him either in the Upperworld or in Hades. When you come face to face with the individual you will see there is no escape from punishment for criminal acts. Each individual knows the crimes that have been committed. One may escape in the Upperworld trial by peers or colleagues but final confrontation with the self is assured in the front hall of Hades."

These utterances of the voice threw me back once more down memory lane. The voice was telling me that there was no escape from wrongdoing no matter how trivial. The only consolation was that the punishment could be small or large depending on the gravity of the wrongdoing. I myself started to wonder and although I remembered beyond my days at Queen's I chose to identify only those events which occurred during my time at Queen's. What punishment would be meted out to me for taking the bicycle of one of the F-ss twins and riding home for lunch without his knowledge? It was only a few times when I was in 2A that I did it. What of the time I went to the horse-races with my friend M.O.? I remember that it was in October of 1948. M.O. and I went to Durban Park after a cricket game one Saturday. We each had two shillings. Whilst walking around the turf we saw the three card game being played where in order to win one has to identify the card bearing white as opposed to the other two cards which were black. I put one of my shillings on a card feeling quite certain that my eyes were the sharpest at the turf and I would pick the white card. Lo and behold I lost! I then put my other shilling on a card in the next game and I lost again. In an effort to regain my two shillings I asked M.O. to lend me one of his and that when I won I would give it back to him, needless to say I lost that too! M.O. looked worried and there was a fear upon his face which told me that he could not return home without his two shillings. Once more in desperation I asked him to lend me his other shilling and told him that when I won I would give him his two shillings and we would proceed homewards. M.O. having given me the second shilling entrenched my view that he was truly a friend as he exposed himself to whatever punishment lay ahead when he returned home if I did not win. Need I tell you that I lost that shilling too! What a miserable day that was! To this day I never found out what happened when he returned home but I eventually repaid him his two shillings. It took almost three weeks. I promised myself that never again would I play the three card game. The memory of that event always returns when I see people playing the game with regular playing cards. I have seen this so many times on the streets of New York. I thought of the punishment I would have to endure when it was my turn to enter the forechamber.

"Traveller, let us move on. There will be no punishment for what you did. You have learnt your lesson and you have never repeated playing the game!" How did this voice know what I was thinking? No doubt the voice was knowledgeable of my intent when I faced the one I sought. The voice had warned that I must adhere to the truth or honest speculation. This I must do. The thought of being guilty of falsehood and its subsequent punishment was foremost in my mind. I could not just accost the subject. I had to have a sound basis for addressing him when we met.

It was then that I remembered I could use the book and some papers I was carrying in my brown envelope. I would quote from the book passages from the speeches of the objective in addressing him. In 1970 two misguided gentlemen co-edited a book entitled *A Destiny to Mould*, it being selected discourses by the Prime Minister of Guyana, Forbes Burnham. I say the gentlemen were misguided since they took upon themselves to believe sincerely in the words that Burnham uttered, falling prey to his eloquent oratory and failing to delve deeper into the nature of the man. Allow me to quote them:

He has met with courage and is tackling with imagination and inventiveness almost all the problems that face the Third World and many of the problems that plague the whole world.

The task before Forbes Burnham is still a gigantic one, but those of us who have come to know him and love him over the years look forward with eagerness to a future full of promise under his leadership.[1]

Through some means Burnham was able to persuade these two gentlemen to compile in a book a collection of speeches, statements and broadcasts made by him. I imagine that, in their later years when they saw what was happening to Guyana, their love faded away. Those gentlemen, who both grew up in Guyana, cannot deny that Guyana suffered at the hands of Burnham, his inventiveness and imagination. At the time of co-editing the book they could not see what dismal future lay in store. Yet, an expression of gratitude is due the gentlemen since without their compilation there would be no record to compare the speeches made then and later events which took place. If the book *A Destiny to Mould* is allowed to stand in the library all by itself as part of Guyana's history future readers will feel that Guyana had a great leader and was well-placed among the nations of the world. It never was so. It is a country that has suffered grievously through political evil. There is no doubt that the Burnham speeches and statements are moving and had Burnham achieved a fraction of what was said in them Guyana would have been better off, but this was not to be. The book reminds me of the mythical Trojan war when the Greeks entered Troy in a wooden horse. Quite spectacular on the outside but in the core there was disaster. Burnham's honey-coated speeches were soothing to the ear. Most of them were unpublished. They were delivered with colourful and flawless oratory but like a Burberry mackintosh they cloaked the treacherous and deceitful intentions that lay silent in his mind. Reading the speeches in his book brought back to my memory the age old words, 'Oh what a tangled web we weave when first we practise to deceive'. It also made me remember the words of my good friend A.G. from Jamaica when he said

---

[1] p.xxxiv

to me one day at the University of Manitoba in 1961, *Jayme, this is what 'im say, but man this is what 'im do!* The contents of the speeches promised abundant prosperity and that good things were to be done for Guyana, but in actual fact Guyana endured catastrophic experiences. What A.G. did not know was that in the desire for power, truth and honesty were elusive coming from a slippery tongue and when the quest was for absolute power the elusiveness was more mercurial. For some men, knowingly, this is the only route.

Burnham wanted to be the champion of the small man. He ended up being the one to put the small man in endless earthly chains, so much so that the small man in Guyana is now shackled throughout life. His whole way of living has been changed, not for the better but for the worse. The small man has been placed in a vortex, and is unable to reach the top. Burnham renamed Guyana calling it the Cooperative Republic of Guyana. Through the mechanism of the cooperative he expected to make the small man a real man. I cite from a speech made on 24th August, 1969, when he addressed the People's National Congress Regional Conference in Georgetown under the caption 'The Cooperative Republic', *You have been told by party leaders that the cooperative is the means through which the SMALL MAN CAN BECOME A REAL MAN, the means through which the small man can participate fully in the economic life of the nation and the means through which the small man can play a predominant part in the workings of the economy.*[1] This was the first time that I realized that the small man of Guyana was not a real man. I had heard in Guyana the term 'real man' mentioned in another sphere but its concept was more to do with complaints from women who found their men wanting in some form or other. Further in the same speech he said, *The small man will, through the cooperative, be able to own large and substantial business enterprises and make decisions which will materially*

---

[1] p.157

effect the direction which the economy takes and where the country goes. In the Cooperative Republic we will be no longer 'drawers of water and hewers of wood.'[1] Burnham's legacy illustrated that the Guyanese people could hardly get good water to drink and Mrs Viola Burnham told the people to go back to coal pots which meant the use of wood and coals. The only thing that the small man was able to own was himself. At times of voting even this was forfeited. The state became the controller of the economy. A country which was as modern as it could be in the fifties and early sixties was being pushed back. As to how the country went the small man can take solace in, apart from not shouting out, knowing that he was not responsible for the complete wrecking of the economy and the Cooperative Republic. Efforts to help the small man were only hearsay, for example, when the small farmer took his pigs to the Guyana Marketing Corporation to sell, the pigs reared by Mrs Viola Burnham would be bought first and the quota was soon taken up so that some farmers did not get their pigs sold. When questioned about it Burnham would reply, "My wife's pork is of a better quality". Those with a very comfortable living found no shame in depriving the small man of a livelihood. They prospered in his name and over his back.

When I was very young I remember reading a nursery rhyme called Humpty Dumpty. My visual recollection of Humpty Dumpty was of a large egg with two arms and two small legs sitting on a wall. It was only when I became a grown man that I would recognise the significance of the rhyme which if memory serves me right went like this:

Humpty Dumpty sat on a wall.
Humpty Dumpty had a great fall;
All the King's horses,
And all the King's men
Could not put Humpty Dumpty together again!

---

[1] p.159

Burnham in his governing of Guyana from 1964 to 1985 would go to prove the logic in that nursery rhyme of early childhood, for Guyana has certainly fallen and in its present broken state cannot be put back again to its former prosperous state. There is no other place in the world that could compete for the title Humpty Dumpty since Guyana could never again become that place that was in retrospect, prior to Burnham's ascent to government, my paradise.

On coming to power Burnham inherited an able and capable civil service, a literate population, a country with resources and a people ready to embark on the road to nationhood and prosperity through hard work and dedication. Queen's at the time, I would venture to say, could be regarded as the top secondary school in the British colonial empire. Scholars and able students were leaving eager to further their education and to return home to fulfil their dreams. Most of those who left returned after finishing their studies. British Guiana was poised to achieve great things and only leadership of some quality was necessary. Unfortunately, this was not afforded the country since the quest for absolute personal power was foremost in Burnham's mind. Having taken hold of men and resources he failed to perform. Successful progress in nation building and development would require the combined efforts of the two main racial groups in existence – East Indians and Africans. Burnham's plans and motives would instead of bringing harmony create a further division of the two groups, and the methods he used to retain and control power shattered the very foundation upon which nationhood is built. Under his guidance the country embarked on a total economic collapse. On the question of personal achievement Burnham satisfied his lifelong ambition of being an overseer on a horse and carrying a whip. He assumed the mantle of the slave drivers and masters of indentured servants as he rode his horse on an estate, ironically named Hope, in the Belfield area on the East Coast of Guyana. For those who were subject to this humiliation it was a harsh life. The book *A Destiny to Mould* would therefore give me a starting point for my purpose. I would quote from the book and then pose my questions and concerns. I would adhere to the truth and satisfy honest speculation.

"Well done Traveller! You have found a way to achieve your goal, we proceed to the forechamber!" At this point I addressed the voice for the first time, saying, "Voice of unquenchable knowledge, tell me before we enter this dreaded place that you have described, who are you and why do you take an interest in me?"

The voice replied, "I am your divine guardian and as proof I ask you to recall some occasions and how close you yourself came to the forechamber. Do you remember the time as a child when you were kicked by a cow in the shed and developed an abscess behind your left ear? Do you recall the events in Den Amstel when you were about to enter the heart of the coconut tree and saw the green parrot snake? Do you remember falling from the genip tree in Lamaha Street and almost being impaled on the fence? Do you remember your first visit to Bartica in 1954 when you almost drowned? Do you recall the running of Itanime Falls in the Essequibo River in 1958? Do you recall on that same trip the bushmaster snake passing under your spout when you were relieving yourself one morning soon after waking up? I could recall many more but all you need to know is that I was there at each and every one of those incidents. Need you ask who I am?

"I must caution you about your return from Hades. When you hear the singing of a hymn in the auditorium it will be the signal for you to return. As you leave the subject walk backwards in a straight line. Keep your eyes on the subject and retreat. If you do not heed this caution your safe return is not guaranteed and perhaps you may find yourself not in the same hall but in another hall of Hades. Do not forget and overstay your visit. Remember the hymn." This caution had me worried as I was not sure that I would be able to keep still. I had read the story of Lot's wife in the Bible when she was told not to look back when Sodom and Gomorrah were being destroyed. She did look back and was turned into a pillar of salt. What would happen to me if I did not heed the instructions? I wanted to make the visit to the Underworld to see Forbes Burnham and I told myself that I would keep my head straight as if I were back with the Cadets at Queen's. The training and discipline learnt in the Cadet Corps would see me through. When I reflect back Queen's really did give one a well-rounded education. Down in the Underworld Burnham could do me no harm as he would be powerless and speechless.

Chapter Three

I remembered all of the occasions the voice spoke about and upon hearing its recollections I felt safe and assured. The running of Itanime Falls on the Essequibo River is most vivid in my memory as it was a very dangerous adventure. It was in late April of 1958. I recall travelling towards Bartica on the Essequibo River having left the camp site at Muruwa River. At the top of Itanime Falls the boat was unloaded and its contents carried by the workers to the bottom of the Falls using a passage that was already cut. The boat would run the Falls. I was the only passenger in the boat with Captain Singh, John Osborne, in charge of the outboard motor, and Joe Lynch, master bowman. I had heard about Itanime and its dangers. Many boats have crashed there and many lives have been lost, so much so that a folk song has been composed about it. I remember the river flowing fast and the narrow channel which we had to use although the river was very wide at this point. And I remember those protruding rocks which flanked both sides of the chosen channel. A single error by Joe and we would all have gone to Hades. Joe was masterful with the oar and he always moved the oar from side to side with flair. I recall when the run was finished and I saw the geologist in charge, Maurice Carter, who after being told that I ran the Falls with Captain Singh, told me that he was going to tell my mother. He knew how dangerous it was. Besides being a bowman, Joe, a black Guyanese, was also a fantastic archer, as he always brought to camp a good quantity of Pacu fish which he shot with his bow and arrow at the top of the rapids. He was so skilled in his art that if you did not know him you would not have believed that he was not an Amerindian. Also on that particular trip I remember climbing to the top of the Kumuti mountain and viewing the scenery from there. I could not help but think how beautiful this country was. It was Easter Monday, 1958, when I made that climb. So many things happened on that trip that reminded me of Bomba, the jungle boy who was the main character in the Bomba books which I borrowed from the library at Queen's and read after classes.

The voice, knowing about those many experiences, told me I was in good hands. All fear vanished. There was no need to question the voice again. I was convinced that the voice was knowledgeable about my whole life and must be a guardian of some sort. I thought of the voice's knowledge of the speech that I wanted to make in 1991 when there would be free and fair elections at the next general election in Guyana in 1992 and when it was permitted for one to speak freely and not worry about being dismissed or victimised. I was going to speak as leader of the Party of National Unity (PNU), pronounced p-new, a new political party endeavouring to win the next elections. The speech in mind was to be as follows:

Fellow Guyanese, I thank you for giving me the opportunity to address you. If I am too harsh in this maiden speech bear with me, for the damage done by the PNC does not give me the chance to be forgiving. Representatives of the People's National Congress have challenged the opposition to come up with a programme telling us that their party is the only party that can solve the problems of this country – let me tell you something, the PNC has created the problems of this country, and let me tell you something else, they are the only party that do not know how to solve anything! Never in the history of any country has a political party done so much destruction and harm as the PNC has done to

Guyana in peacetime – yes, peacetime! For since their access to power in December 1964 there has never been an incident of disruption as witnessed during the period 1961-1964.

We the opposition have a positive programme for the restoration of our country. We acknowledge that it is a most difficult task, for what the PNC has done in the last twenty-seven years is difficult to comprehend. If those who have been dead since 1964 can get a chance to have one look again at this country today they would double their blessings for being allowed to escape the horrors of the past twenty-seven years. Guyanese have had to endure so many hardships and such degradation that I am sure that the only time they were at peace was when they were fast asleep. On awakening they faced days of drudgery – endless queues (now called guylines) for essentials and commodities, fuel shortages, electricity cuts, coloured water and numerous deprivations. We were even told that we should abandon our electric, gas and kerosene stoves and go back to coal pots. The audacity! But friends, I would like to take a short journey into history.

This beloved country of ours, Guyana – bounded by sea and land – was once a jewel of the British Commonwealth. At the time of the taking of power, the PNC inherited a country that was known for its intellectual capabilities, a country that could boast of the birth of scholars in the Commonwealth whose abilities, when measured, were so great, that, given a normal development, this country would have been able not only to put a man on the moon but to have its own satellite. We have sons of Guyana abroad who work in these fields. Don't you forget that!

When Forbes Burnham came into power he had at his disposal a country endowed with resources, intellectual manpower, skills, and a people determined to progress and advance along with the world. We were about to embark on our own and we were prepared to accept the challenges that were presented to a young, undeveloped nation. Unfortunately, we had the wrong captain and in a short period of time we started to lose key players in the team. Guyana, beloved Guyana, is more fortunate than many countries. Let us examine her from top to bottom. Bordered by the Atlantic Ocean she finds herself endowed with seafood in abundance and her land has never been threatened by hurricanes and tidal waves. Her coastland has lands capable of producing rice, sugar, coconuts, and abundant fruits and vegetables. Inland she is famous for her bauxite and for her hardwood timber and cattle in savannah lands. To crown it all, she has gold, and diamonds, many rivers and the splendour of Kaieteur in the interior.

Friends, not many countries can boast of such resources. So what was her problem? The PNC! Yes, the People's National Catastrophe! The PNC was not even aware of her richness, for were they aware, this country could have been the Switzerland of the Americas – with a high standard of living and a good life. The most difficult task that would have confronted us was obtaining and creating a fair immigration policy, since we would have been inundated with people wanting to come here to live! Instead, emigration is one of our better exports! Guyana is too complex a country for members of the PNC to appreciate, much less to govern. Today, Guyana stands ruined and is in a state of desperation. When we think of her position tears come pouring down and there is nothing we can do at the moment because the perpetrators of her demise and calamitous state are still in power and telling us and themselves that they are the only ones who can take her out of this mess. Friends, if these people remain in power, I suggest you start learning to swim and/or to fly, because this place will not be fit to live in. If the PNC is not defeated in the forthcoming election they will be in power forever.

Today, there is so much talk of divestment – divestment here, divestment there! There is only one divestment that is needed, the divestment of the PNC from running the affairs of the people of Guyana. But Friends, I know that on Election Day with your ballots which will be counted fair and square this time you will divest the PNC from government and it would be a one hundred per cent divestment, not 50/50. The people would have responded!

The election has been postponed because of the exposure of the intentions of the PNC to have an electoral list crowded with persons unknown, and in some cases persons already dead! One famous personality long dead turned up on the list with three residences! It was a disgrace to the authorities to have Mr Jimmy Carter of the United States of America urging that a new voters' list be prepared and also to have him convince Prezi Desi that there is no difficulty in counting the votes at the polling station. Friends, let me tell you this: If the PNC have any thoughts of rigging this forthcoming election, they had better forget it. The time for change is at hand, and there is nothing that can stop that. Look at this country today and tell me that if you were in full possession of your faculties and you had a conscience, what reason would there be to vote for the PNC? Would you like to continue suffering? I tell you my Friends, even members of the PNC would vote for some other Party! The ruination brought to this country by the PNC is so formidable that there will be plenty of work for us to do together for a long time. The task ahead is an uphill one, but rebuild we will. Yes, upon *the removal of this cancer from our midsts we shall recover.*

Recently, when it was suggested that Mr Ashton Chase be nominated as the consensus candidate for President, The Chronicle *newspaper took it upon itself to go into history, and to raise an issue of Green versus Chase. I urge* The Chronicle *if it desires to delve into history to go back to the days when this country flourished, when we had a democratic society, when there was no shortage of food, pharmaceuticals, medical care and all the good things of life; when there was no fuss about electoral lists. If* The Chronicle *wants to be fair, let it go back and tell us of its competition –* The Graphic, The Argosy, *and* The Evening Post. *Let it tell us about when this little country had four daily newspapers. Let* The Chronicle *tell the young people of this country how rich their heritage was – tell them of the railway, the first in South America; tell them of the high production of rice and sugar; tell them of the smiling faces of the people. Tell them that when a person voted the ballot was counted for the individual or party voted for. Tell them that mail was never tampered with as it is today! If* The Chronicle *wants to go the route of Green versus Chase, let it tell of the Granada TV Programme of 1968 which showed a field full of livestock in England and where Guyanese people were supposed to be living for the overseas votes.*

Friends, I do not believe we have been forsaken! We have been going through a time of hardship for twenty-seven years, but it will soon be over. With the help of God and the powers that be in this world of developed and underdeveloped nations, we shall overcome. We shall have in the future – jobs, electricity, clear water to drink and cook, a good educational system, a health care system to look after the young, old and the afflicted, plus more. We shall produce more sugar, more rice, and more top quality bauxite. We shall organise for production and consequently the betterment of our people. All of this would be possible because we shall be rid of the PNC – the People's National Catastrophe! Prezi Desi and his group know that they have been a catastrophe. In the quest for and the retention of power the PNC has deprived Guyanese of basic freedoms and have failed to deliver jobs, food, housing, education and good health to the people of this country. They have failed miserably, to such an extent that they have made the Guyana dollar go the route of a precipice. Imagine $125 Guyana dollars for $1 US Dollar; $60 Guyana Dollar for $1 Barbados dollar; $45 Guyana for $1 Eastern Caribbean dollar, and we all belong to Caricom. What a disgrace!

Friends, the task ahead is not easy since most of our skilled people have been driven away from this country. The PNC through its system of governing has caused many good people to leave this country to seek a better life elsewhere. Today Guyanese citizens adorn the offices of many companies in foreign lands. They carve a name out for themselves and they are a credit to their employers. Those who have ventured out on their own, perform outstandingly well. Perhaps had not the PNC driven them away they would not have prospered so well. In an effort to do well outside they have been forced to put forward their best and they have done this creditably. Can we get them back? Maybe! But we must move ahead without them. We have to start rebuilding without them, we have to start digging in and throwing out!

The leaders of the PNC who have placed us in this unenviable position are still there and there is nothing on the horizon which indicates that their thinking has changed. It is those same people who got us into this mess who still expect to be there. What would they do *differently? The PNC has been in power for so long that they do not know anything else but being in power, and therein lies the difficulty. They cannot come up with anything new since they are incapable of doing so. They have been incapable and incompetent for the last twenty-seven years. The PNC has said that the ERP – Entirely Reversed Policy – will bring back Guyana to prosperity. My Friends, the Economic Recovery Programme espoused by the PNC cannot get us back anywhere without the confidence of our people! You, Friends, must have confidence in the PNC and I say that confidence is not visible. For almost three decades we have suffered at the hands of the PNC! The PNC was so arrogant and domineering that they told us that the Party was paramount. Look what paramountcy has done to us? Look around Friends, and tell me if you have ever witnessed so much despair, unhappiness, and symptoms of depression? Paramountcy has led to the disenfranchisement of a whole nation. With the assistance of the police and the army, they have constantly rigged the elections and the electoral lists, since 1968 the Guyanese people have been deprived of the vote – the most important means of determining a government. Without the vote have you really got a say in your country? The ability to vote in, or out, any party is your prerogative. Only you the people can make that decision! In the past the decision has been made for you and as you look around you see what it has done to this country – left it limp like wilted spinach on a hot sunny day. But, my Friends, you are not dead and you still have the opportunity to get rid of this cancer that has caused us so much pain and distress. Guyana, a most beautiful country with a kind and honest people, stands today at the bottom of the world's economic ladder. We have been brought to our knees. Our better welfare and development as a nation depended on their success and as you have witnessed they have been failures. Hopefully, we are going to crawl and then walk upright. Riddance of the People's National Catastrophe will give us the encouragement and strength we need. We will be rid of them once and for all. The objective of us the opposition is to get the PNC out of office and out of government. The only thing that really matters is getting them out – voting them out and sweeping them out. We will have back our country and we will put in place the systems that make a nation proud. We will look after the young, the old and the meek. We will see to it that there are job provisions, food, housing, clothing, education, a dependable healthcare system, recreation facilities, and an infrastructure that will allow us to stand proud, firstly in the Caribbean, and then in the world. We hold the key (raising the symbol of a key) to your future development and success. We were once a respected people and we will become so again. The only thing that stands between success and the future is the People's National Catastrophe – the PNC – and you my Friends will help us to get rid of them. Vote for the key. Thank you.*

The speech was never made since the party was never formed. The reason for wanting to enter into politics was not so much to become a political leader but to save the spirit, nay soul, of the nation as so much despair had taken hold of the people and they needed to be guided back to a position of hope. I did not believe that the parties that were in existence had any answers in providing that hope. To my mind none of the political parties knew what was involved in building a nation. Their only aspiration was gaining political power. To me the two major political parties have never exhibited any political ability despite the country having good people and abundant natural resources. When it came to moving the country forward it seemed to me as if they were faced with a solid wall.

They did not know what to do or how to go about achieving success. But that was then. Subsequent results of the elections in October 1992 indicated that the Guyanese people were still voting along racial lines and it further convinced me that Burnham's legacy would remain in place for a very long time. My own view is that without national unity Guyana will not go forward and is doomed to be a place of mere existence. This will only change when the people begin to regard themselves as Guyanese and not as East Indians or Africans, forgetting their initial origins and giving their allegiance to Guyana. This does not mean that they have to forget their ancestry but it does mean that Guyana must be regarded as their homeland and that of their descendants. Guyana is their founding place. They must then listen to what is being offered by political aspirants regardless of their ethnic origins and choose after careful scrutiny. Voting along racial lines will only keep the country in a state of distrust and it will be a perpetual impediment to true progress.

"Traveller! Behold we are entering the forechamber. You will soon see the man you seek. Initially, you will feel uncomfortable because of the heat and foul smell of the place, but this will not be for long and will pass in a few seconds. It is to remind you of the unpleasantness of this abode." During my journey to this part of Hades we passed through winding passages and I could hear eerie cries and sounds of the shadows of human beings placed in varying positions of discomfort.

As we entered the forechamber of the halls of Hades, I could feel the intense heat and although it was only for a few seconds I wished that I were at the North Pole, for only there would I feel comfortable! The heat was as intense, if not more so, as the heat encountered in the close environment of steel-making furnaces. I know this because I have toured many steel plants as part of my job. The foul smell reminded me of the mercaptans in chemistry exercises. These are gases that are very malodorous and the smell of rotten eggs do not compare. At this point I longed for the smell of Limacol, the freshness of a breeze in a bottle: Limacol, that pleasant smelling evaporative liquid produced by the Guyana Pharmaceutical Corporation. Fortunately, as promised, the foul smell and the heat were short-lived, but for those who abide in this section of Hades, this is surely a maddening punishment. I recalled the voice telling me of crawling creatures, flying insects, and numerous monsters. They were all visible as we progressed further into the forechamber. My thoughts were of Aeneas when he visited the Underworld, but unlike me he had to pick a golden bough as a gift for Proserpine, the Queen of Hades, before he would be allowed to cross the river Styx in the boat of grim and aged Charon. I was spared this since my visitor was bound to the front of Hades and could go no further. His deeds during his life in the Upperworld precluded him from gaining access to the grounds beyond the Stygian Stream. The landscape in Burnham's abode was desolate and barren. It was a murky realm. The shadows which dwell here are not allowed to encounter any forms of beauty. Not visible are any streams, nor other bodies of water, nor is there any vegetation. It was an abode which was distinctly opposite to the Elysian Fields where the good of mankind dwell and where it is a land of joy and happiness, peaceful without harsh weather and there is no need or want.

Chapter Four

At last I saw the apparition of Burnham, barely recognisable since surrounding his body were numerous articles and objects. He was standing on a four-legged stool. As I came closer my vision became clearer and I could see around his neck was a noose of sturdy chain wrought in steel which hung from a scaffold attached to a partially enclosed cubicle which had the appearance of a voting booth. I could see only one ballot box in the cubicle. Beside the stool I could see three discarded ballot boxes. On the scaffold facing me was marked in bold letters "DISENFRANCHISE". This I gathered was perhaps the most serious of all offences since it simulated a hanging. The elections which were held in Guyana in the years 1968, 1973, 1980, and 1985 coupled with a Constitutional Referendum in 1980 were all massively rigged. Some Guyanese who protested the removal of ballot boxes by members of the Guyana Defence Force were killed in their efforts. The hanging image represented the ultimate punishment for the rigging of elections and the loss of lives of innocent people who were only trying to protect their rights. This crime was considered very serious since rigging undermined the very foundation of democracy and of nationhood. The vote was the peaceful mechanism of choice of the people and its important exercise was crucial to the society. The forfeiture and seizure after voting of the ballot boxes were recognised as extremely criminal acts. If the theft of the people's votes was not a violation of human rights, then what is?

Continuing my observations, I recognised a building modelled after the old Queen's College in Brickdam resting on his head. The weight of it I could not tell, but I am sure it was proportionate for the occasion. He was educated in this building when he attended Queen's. Seeing him this way reminded me of those vendors who carried their wares on top of their heads when going to market. Around his left arm was an object which had the appearance of a dentist's chair. On it I could barely see the markings V.T.. Protruding from his back I saw an object which looked like a spear bearing the boldly written word: "DARKE". Next to this spear was a rifle and on its handle I recognised the name "McLEOD". Around his neck was a chain made of barbed wire and on the chain there were several miniature objects hanging like charms on a bracelet. I recognised an object looking like a walkie-talkie and it was labelled "RODNEY". I saw a miniature model of the Lady Thompson Ward at the Georgetown Hospital, models of the waterworks building in Vlissengen Road, the electricity works at Kingston, the Supreme Court, the post office building, and of a walking dragline similar to the one used for mining bauxite at the Linden Mine sites. There were other objects, but smaller. As I got much closer I could see sheets of paper with a list of names embracing the stool. This I believed to be a voters' list; all of the electoral lists since the first rigging in 1968, and onwards, included names of non-existent persons both at home and abroad. There was a programme produced by Granada Television which showed fields of horses and cows and those sites were given as the residences of overseas Guyanese voters. This image of a stool with voters' list and Burnham standing on top was mirroring his ascent to power over the Guyanese people through contrived electoral lists and fraudulent voting. Removal of the stool would bring finality through the noose and thus give relief to the people of Guyana. It was Burnham who said on 18th November, 1962, at the Parade Ground in Georgetown, *It seems to me, I may be wrong, but I have never been so sure in my life of anything, that he who seeks to support an electoral system which robs some political parties of the number of seats to which their popular votes entitle them has a tremendous onus placed upon him to justify such an electoral system. In other words, you have placed upon you the onus of justifying electoral theft...*[1] We all know that stealing is a crime. In Hades' halls punishment was being administered.

Observation of the wire chain with its appendages was reminiscent of Marley's ghost in Charles Dickens' *A Christmas Carol.* As I recall Marley's ghost had a long chain clasped about his waist and it was made of cash boxes, keys, padlocks, ledgers, deeds and heavy purses wrought in steel. The items were all associated with his vocation and workplace. I gathered, therefore, that the labelled items and other objects seen about Burnham were directly or indirectly associated with him in various ways. I remember also that in Dickens' novel Marley was regarded as having no bowels (intestinal fortitude). In Burnham's case, however, it could not be said that he had no bowels. Quite the contrary, Burnham was bold and aggressive. A short testimony to his boldness can be grasped from his address before His Royal Highness the Duke of Kent when the Constitutional Instruments for Guyana were being presented on May 26th, 1966. The speech appears in his book:

After 150 years of British rule, and in some cases, misrule, we are now independent. But we harbour no bitterness. Bitterness, we feel is for children and the intellectually under-developed. It is difficult, nay impossible, to change the facts of past history and in the circumstances, though we welcome with enthusiasm our new status, we are prepared not to spend the time ahead of us abusing those who once dictated to us but rather to seek means of cooperating with them to our mutual advantage – shall I say, self interest.[2] This was just a small example of the boldness of the man.

---

[1] p.83
[2] p.xiii

Bowels or not, the bodiless figure facing me was one of submission. It was quite obvious if the chain with its appendages coupled with a noose were symbolic of the burdens that have to be borne in the afterlife, that Burnham was under tremendous strain. Marley's crimes were small in comparison. Marley had only been miserly and kept his wealth to himself. In simple terms he was not a generous man. The indications in the case of Burnham were, however, that his crimes were against people and institutions and thus much more serious. The only time I remember seeing Burnham so adorned was during his earthly life when, as Commander-in-Chief, he dressed in full military uniform – braids, stars and all the military paraphernalia. Photographs in that costume reminded me of Idi Amin Dada, the Ugandan eliminator of human lives. Colourful as he was in the Upperworld, down here the encumbrances were real.

"Traveller! The deeds committed by your objective are considered more serious because he was a man of the law. By training and development he was a representative of the Rule of Law. His was a vocation which prepares one to uphold the law, enforce the law, and give judgement based upon the law. Instead he chose to be above the law. Less harsh treatment is meted out to those who err. But officers of the law are not spared. From the law justice is expected. Right must be triumphant and without the Rule of Law there is no society. The forsaking of truth and honesty invites a severity of great magnitude."

This caution by the voice replaced any sympathetic feelings that may have been developing for the tortured figure. The Rule of Law and its upholding were fundamental. Revelations of the voice sent me back immediately to two excerpts from Burnham's speeches. The first was an excerpt from a speech made in the Legislative Assembly on 1st March, 1962, *So far as I am aware a plot to assassinate or kill any person is still a criminal offence punishable under chapter 10 of the Laws of*

British Guiana.[1] To this day that law is still applicable. Yet, when certain events took place during the Burnham maladministration, nothing was ever done. The second excerpt was from a speech on 28th August, 1969, in the National Assembly, after winning the first rigged General Election.

...Traditionally, our final Court of Appeal has been our Majesty in Council or the Judicial Committee of the Privy Council. Lest there be any illusions, lest there be any suggestions, that the cards were not put on the table, and today is the day for putting the cards on the table, let me first observe that there is an inherent inconsistency behind Guyana becoming a republic and Guyana still having Her Majesty's Privy Council, the Judicial Committee or what have you, as the final Court of Appeal.

To continue to have the Judicial Committee of the Privy Council as the final Court of Appeal is to admit to our inferiority which our erstwhile masters have attempted to instill in us, is to admit that we are incapable of finding within the boundaries of our country such legal talent and such sense of justice as would lead us to leave the final arbitrament of matters legal to our fellow Guyanese.

Far be it from me, Mr Speaker, to suggest that the Judicial Committee of the Privy Council does not consist of eminent lawyers. Far be it from me to attempt to suggest that it might not be the fount of justice, but far be it from me, a nationalist, to tolerate this inconsistency, this incongruity so far as I have any power to bring it to an end. Those who have ears to hear, let them hear.

Whatever, may be our differences, there cannot be differences between the majority in this House as to the suitability, desirability, of having a British court decide for us in Guyana. Whatever may be our differences, I would hope and expect that the same overwhelming majority which will pass this resolution will pass any proposed amendment to the constitution

---

[1] p.27

brought to let the right of appeal inhere in the Court of Appeal of Guyana.[1]

The abandonment of the Privy council as the final Court of Appeal led to many judgements thereafter in the Court of Appeal of Guyana which left one side of contestants dissatisfied one way or another. However, to my mind the most glaring of all is the case brought by one Captain Chichester who was fighting for his pension after thirty years of service in the Transport and Harbours Department, only to be told by the highest Court in the land that "receipt of a pension was a privilege of the State and not a right". This case has been reported in the West Indian Law Reports of 1970. Apparently, shortly before his retirement Captain Chichester had an accident with the ferry boat that he captained and this earned him the wrath of Burnham. He was deprived of his pension as punishment and that judgement still stands today and has never been repealed by Parliament. In other words, when my own time comes I may not get a pension. I sincerely believe that a judgement of this nature would never have been handed down by members of the Judicial Committee of the Privy Council. Permit me to say that in most civilised societies officials of the government seek an individual out, even in distant lands, to see that a pension, when due, is received. With Burnham this could never have been.

The retention of the Privy Council was not to slight legal luminaries in Guyanese society, but the society was so small and manipulation was always possible so that true justice was never quite assured. In presenting a case to the Law Lords of the Privy Council only the law would be considered. The esteemed judges sitting on the panel do not know the litigants. Captain Chichester, like Mrs Olivia Casey Jaundoo, would not have been known to them, only the legal issues raised. There were many who longed for an appeal to the Privy Council but this possibility was non-existent. Had Captain Chichester been

---

[1] p.71

able to appeal to the Privy Council their Lordships would have allowed his appeal, adding that the Respondent (Government) bear all costs for the present appeal and in the court below. It would have been their way of sending a message to the Judges of the perverse decision. I mention Mrs Jaundoo as this was one of the last civil appeal cases from the Courts of Guyana to the Privy Council. In that matter the Burnham Government attempted to take the property of Mrs Jaundoo without paying compensation. On appeal by Mrs Jaundoo, their Lordships had no hesitation in allowing the appeal and awarding costs to the Appellant. Burnham's removal of the Privy Council eliminated the last recourse to justice and strengthened his stronghold on the Guyanese people. There were some who welcomed his decision but as time passed and it was revealed that nothing could be challenged successfully since *HE* was the final Court of Appeal they lamented. Burnham had deified himself and there were no further avenues of recourse. He knew what he was doing and the Privy Council was perhaps the main item for elimination. It was the only place where Justice and its partner Hope resided.

As I came much closer to the tortured apparition I recalled seeing a motion picture entitled *The Picture of Dorian Gray*, based on the book of the same name by Oscar Wilde. The closeness of the chain and the various objects brought back memories of Dorian Gray whose portrait became embedded with all the crimes he committed, the young man himself remaining ever youthful and never growing old. Whatever misdeeds were committed resulted in an etching on the portrait. The portrait was locked away from sight. No one knew why Gray remained ever youthful. However, when he died the etchings disappeared and the painting resumed its normal state. However, the once youthful man looked aged, gruesome and horrible. This was the picture before me.

I knew this man prior to his ascent to the seat of power in Guyana. This was a man who visited our home and I remembered him telling my mother, "Mrs Ramsahoye, don't call me Mr Burnham, call me Odo". I do not know if, after experiencing life under Burnham, she said that he should have called himself 'Dodo'. She was a very witty woman. He had tea on many occasions in our home in Charlotte Street. I myself used to visit his law office to give him news of the progress of my brother Fenton who was studying for his Ph.D. in Law at the London School of Economics during 1957 to 1959. Both of them were members of the same law firm, Clarke and Martin, for a short while. I say short, because my brother left the firm to set up his own practice. He had found himself burdened with most of the legal work whilst Burnham went in search of the route to power which when achieved would allow him to control all, to rule all and to dictate to all. I knew the legal workload was partly responsible but the clincher to the departure was when Burnham returned from England and turned up during the Test match being played between the West Indies and England at Bourda in March of 1960 and said that he did not want independence under Jagan. That was the straw that broke the camel's back. It caused my brother to join the PPP soon after. All colonials wanted independence irrespective of who was the leader of the government.

Let me tell you that Burnham on earth presented a formidable figure! He was in my view perhaps the most eloquent of public speakers. His oratory was unsurpassed and he was endowed with abundant charisma. On the right side of the law this man could be invincible. When one reads the speeches embodied in *A Destiny to Mould,* and envisages the eloquence of their delivery, there can be no denying that he could be persuasive. Burnham's oratory was not dissimilar to the music which Orpheus sang, accompanied by the strains of his lyre when he visited the Underworld. Orpheus sang so sweetly during his visit there that even the ghosts shed tears. Burnham's words flowed and they were sweeter than syrup made from sugar produced in the county of Demerara[b]. It was always such a joy to listen to him speak at political meetings. I remembered him well in 1952 and 1953. This man was the champion of oratory and I would insist that he had no equal. I could recall crowds attending political meetings of the original PPP and waiting hours to hear this man speak, and when he began to speak the place became silent. Only his voice could be heard. His voice was smooth and he spoke without faltering. Women swooned and men were in awe to hear the English language being used to deflate political opponents. He must have been glad that English was his mother tongue. Lord Byron, Percy Shelley, Jane Austen, Thomas Hardy, Charles Dickens, William Wordsworth, Elizabeth Barrett Browning, Oscar Wilde, Winston Churchill and millions of others spoke the same language. No one wanted to miss a word. Therefore, I say that with such a talent he could have been remembered for good deeds but with his perverse genius he chose dictatorship and totalitarianism, resulting in the destruction of the country's institutions and breeding disenchantment amongst the people. Having snatched absolute power after the 1973 election, Burnham became a different man and in Guyanese parlance he became a snake. He shed his skin and was now looked upon as dangerous and fearful. The speeches embodied in *A Destiny to Mould* which were full of promises and hope, were now illusionary. If I were to name the type of snake based on those that inhabit Guyana I would say he was like the dreaded Haimaralli – beautifully coloured, deadly venomous and never to be trusted. No longer was there any accountability to the people. For the Guyanese people a life that was once sweet became a miserable existence. It was a great betrayal. To many middle class Negro Guyanese and others Burnham became a totally incomprehensible disappointment. Today, Guyana stands in dire straits and is grappling for its very survival.

---

[b] Brown sugar.

I would long to hear him speak in this abysmal place but he was unable to do so since he had lost the mechanism of speech on the operating table at the Georgetown Hospital, an institution that was allowed to fall into a sordid state under his maladministration. Guyanese doctors deserted the hospital and sought refuge in other distant places. Justice saw to it that Burnham did not seek medical attention in a foreign hospital but was admitted to the Lady Thompson Ward of the Georgetown Hospital for a simple operation on his throat. He never regained consciousness after being anaesthetised and death was attributed to cardiac failure. This event took place on the morning of August 6th, 1985.

I remember Burnham speaking to the school body at Queen's in 1953 prior to the holiday break at the end of July. His speech was stirring and his departing words upon the thought of the British Government suspending the constitution of British Guiana were, "...over my dead body." The British suspended the constitution but he lived on for a fraction over thirty-two years, but no one expected him to kill himself over the suspension. I knew he would not be in the front when it came to physical fighting. When others were being charged and jailed he remained untouched, and instead was perhaps their defence lawyer. This was no surprise.

There was no denying that the mighty had fallen. This man who was so powerful in the Upperworld was now helpless in a hall of Hades. I was told by someone a long time ago that this was a man who promoted a private soldier to sergeant immediately on some occasion when Burnham almost lost his life in a helicopter incident. Was this not done by others at other times in other places? This was no precedent but it was a display of power in action. He is reported to have said at the third Biennial conference of the PNC held in 1979, "He who has more power than I, let me have the pleasure of meeting him." Seeing him with the steel noose around his neck, and hanging from the scaffold, told me that he had met the one who had more power, but I was sure that their meeting did not give him any pleasure.

I have said how eloquent and charismatic Burnham was but he was also cruel, ruthless and cunning. Some said he had vision but forgot to mention that it was clouded. He was a tyrant and the people of Guyana were warned by one close to him. This envoy of doom was his sister Jessie and she had warned the Guyanese people in a pamphlet entitled 'Beware My Brother Forbes'. At the time she gave the warning she was in the opposite camp to Burnham and even though there may have been some suspicion that her warning was due to her involvement with the *Opposition*, caution should have been exercised since, as is said, 'blood is thicker than water'. She must have known something about him that would bring about harm to the Guyanese people.

Just as it was possible for a private to be promoted on the spot, so also a minister in Government could fall like Humpty Dumpty. Burnham had all of his ministers of Government sign a letter of resignation and he presented them with it whenever he was desirous of their removal. He only had to insert the date. There was no appeal, no discussion – just swift action. There was one occasion when one of his ministers had applied for a job with the United Nations and approval had to be given by the President of Guyana for the gentleman to be considered for the appointment. Burnham received correspondence from the United Nations requesting his approval for the consideration of the appointment. However, Burnham called the minister to his residence, and during their conversation asked the minister if he was happy in his job. The minister, not knowing that Burnham had a letter from the UN, replied that he was quite happy. Burnham then took out the letter and said, "You do not need this then". He tore up the letter in his presence and then sent him back to work.

As I mention these little episodes, I bear in mind that suitable punishment is meted out to those who stray from the truth and I do not want to find myself fabricating metal charms to adorn my person in that hot and smelly part of the forechamber when my turn comes. What I have recounted were true events.

It was Shakespeare who said in *Julius Caesar*: "The evil that men do lives after them, The good is oft interrèd with their bones." Shakespeare was so right since my observations of the tortured figure exposed those various models and objects but no bones. I am sure there were bones somewhere but I could not see any. Is it that the bones disappear when the evil deeds are so numerous that if there are cancellations of any sort, between good and evil, what remains to be seen are evil symbols? I cannot say, but only the symbols of committed evil were evident on Burnham.

The acquisition of power carries with it an onerous responsibility and it is the use of the acquired power that hurdles one towards the stars or to the infernal depths. To my mind, the desire for power, and in Burnham's case, also the leadership of Guyana, suggests that he was ready to take over the role of father to the people of Guyana. It was his responsibility to see to it that their better welfare was achieved. Instead, we see a shattering of their hopes and dreams and a waste of their birthright. The desire for power surely stems from the mind. It is the mind that signals the need and the brain, willing servant that it is, executes. Whatever we do starts with the mind, whether it may be; for example to become a doctor, lawyer or leader or whatever, the initial seed comes from the mind. It is the mind that pictures the famous painting or work of art and the willing servant ensures its achievement. The mind is infinite and limitless and I would venture to say, except in a lottery or prize drawing, that success is achieved when the brain executes the instructions of the mind. I wondered what kind of picture Burnham envisaged for Guyana. Did he not see that with guidance and astute leadership Guyana would move forward?

"Traveller," the voice chimed in, "do not let your thoughts dwell on philosophy." This was a caution from the voice telling me to get on with my assignment.

As I approached the painful bodiless image of Burnham I heard music in the background and thought it must be a relief for the tortured figure confined to this inhospitable, murky realm. However, the music was that of a calypso, sung by the Mighty Sparrow, the calypso king of the world. I recognised the calypso as 'BG War' and it was sung in 1962. To my ear it was a joy since I enjoyed the music of the Caribbean legend so much. But to Burnham this was torture. How cruel can the authorities of Hades be? Although it was sung for the first time in 1962 and was being heard on the radio when he came to power in 1964, Burnham banned it from being played on both radio stations in Guyana. Sparrow, calypsonian that he is, was noted for creating lyrics of events at the time and his 'BG War' mimicked events that took place in the then British Guiana at the time of riots and disturbances in early 1962. In the background I could hear:

> Well, they drop a hydrogen bomb in BG!
> Lord have mercy!
> They drop a hydrogen bomb in BG!
> Lord have mercy!
> Riot in town Mamma!
> Ah hear the whole place on fire.
> From Kitty to the Waterfront, all that
> Burn down flat, flat, flat!
>
> I ain't care if all ah BG burn down!
> I ain't care if the whole ah Bookers burn down!
> But they'll be putting me out me way
> If they tackle Tiger Bay,
> And burn down me hotel
> Whe' all dem wahbeen does stay.

The music was sweet and infectious. I was more at ease now. But Burnham was no doubt experiencing added agony. In my euphoric state I addressed him thus, "Creator of your own metallic encumbrances, I am afforded an opportunity to address you since I find myself very troubled. It is a most pleasant surprise and I was not prepared for such an encounter. I want to talk about many things but not being prepared you may find me rambling. My name is Jim Ramsahoye and the last time we met face to face was on Boxing Day of 1970 when I visited you at the Belfield retreat. Prior to that you may remember that in 1958-59 we used to go to the Woodbine Hotel for a drink after work when I visited you in Chambers to tell you of the progress of Fenton. Of course, we met whenever you came to visit in Charlotte Street. On that Boxing Day your colleague Hubert Jack was present also. By the way, he is down here now. I did not expect to see you in this position decorated with the tortures of remorse. Your present appearance if it could be immortalised on canvas, would attract the most dreaded fear of all mankind. Just think, in 1964 you were just an ordinary man who practised law and was aspiring to be the political leader of Guyana, and later in that year the birth of a dictator took place. Today, in 1994, I see you here in a most uncomfortable state, woven by your own scheming and actions. As I speak there is a general assembly being held in the auditorium of your *Alma Mater*, Queen's College. Gathered there are alumni from various parts of the world and other well-wishers. They have been celebrating the sesquicentennial anniversary of the school and today's gathering is the culmination of the week's activities. I have not forgotten that tomorrow is an anniversary for you but I have not heard of any preparations in your honour.

"In the auditorium, despite it being an occasion of joy and gladness, it is evident that there is also a great amount of sadness. The visual appearance of the school coupled with the shortage of teaching academia weigh heavily on the celebrating alumni. There have been speeches upon speeches praising the school, reminding the world that it is a school of excellence despite its deterioration and neglect. However, all the speakers have been kind in that no one has mentioned that the demise of the school is as a result of your actions, or inactions. You held in your hands the jewel of all the schools in the underdeveloped British Commonwealth. It is a diamond not unlike the one you held in your hand but this is more valuable. Do you remember the S-k diamond which you bought for $48,000 and could not get more than $32,000 for it because it had a flaw? Just as the loss was painful to you so it is with this gathering, as the loss of stature of the school pains them terribly.

"I know you cannot answer me but your answer rests in a speech of yours. It was you who said in a broadcast to the nation on 27th March 1961, *For us EDUCATION IS THE CORNERSTONE OF EQUALITY and one of the chief instruments for the abolition of snobbery, the removal of discrimination, the development of creative beings and the production of a race of men who will never surrender to mediocrity or dictatorship of any kind.*[1] Did you believe that in 1961 there was still discrimination at the school? Were you thinking in a time warp, intending to let matters take a course wherein the school would be neglected? Or did you fear that this school, which yielded leaders in all fields, would produce a leader who WOULD NOT ACCEPT YOUR INTENDED DICTATORSHIP?

"There were so many reasons for you to keep the school modern and to encourage its growth and development. This was your school, and although you held power over a nation you could not repay the debt you owed to the school. Consider where you would have been and the consequences of not having your education at Queen's! Let me take a guess – not in this place of Hell. There was no denying that there was a need for schools of a similar excellent standard but the answer did not rest with minimising the efforts of QC. Your desire for a

---

[1] p.10

school called the President's College should not have led you to neglect Queen's. You had one jewel already, why not another? Not a replacement. What can replace a diamond? Your President's College should have been complementary to Queen's. After all, from its inception to the first graduate at Advanced Level standard would have taken at least seven years and it would be some time before it established itself like Queen's.

"Scholars who have won the Guyana Scholarship date back as far as 1882 in the school's history. You yourself were the fourth person in the school's history to gain distinctions in English and Latin on winning the Scholarship in 1942. Preceding you were W.R. Pakeman in 1936, C.J. Matthews in 1937, and E.F. Harris in 1940. Your name can be seen on the Honour Board which adorns the auditorium. How could you be so ungrateful to allow the school to deteriorate both physically and with lack of academia? Did you know that the Guyana Scholar of 1949 who is an alumnus was the first Scholar in the British Colonial Empire to get distinctions in Pure and Applied Mathematics, and Physics and Chemistry at one sitting? And did you know that this same feat was repeated in 1960 by another alumnus, and did you also know that the first Guyana Scholar to get three distinctions in Latin, French and Spanish in 1958 was a QC alumnus? His name was H.A. Khan. Records of the school show that it was known for scholars in both the arts and sciences. England has Eton, Harrow and Charterhouse. Guyana has Queen's College, another institution for quality education and development.

"I will not dwell on the school any longer at this time for what is done is done. Efforts must now be made to try to rehabilitate it and steer it on a course similar to that of its former glory. In being thankful I think that one must remember one's parents for giving them life, and following that, gratitude to one's school and those teachers who imparted knowledge and guidance. I cannot say what thanks you have offered to your parents but I know your treatment of the school clearly reflects

that its maintenance and continuance as a school of excellence
was not of your concern."

As I spoke those words the head of the tortured figure
seemed to jolt and there must have been some pressure from the
three storeyed Brickdam building perched on his head. It was
as if the building wanted to say thanks for bringing to light its
treatment by an alumnus. It appeared that the encumbrances
were able to bear down on the figure requiring only the
smallest amount of incentive. Burnham winced as any
movement of the head triggered a movement of the barbed
chain.

The sweet music of Sparrow played on and in the
background I could hear:

They lock up over a thousand people.
Well, that was trouble!
They send for police in the country
To bring unity.
But police and all afraid
Stand up and they watching stores get raid.
Walk in the store, take everything
And when you done, set fire to the building

But I ain't care if the whole ah BG burn down!
I ain't care if all ah Bookers burn down!
But they'll be putting me out me way
If they tackle Tiger Bay
And burn down me hotel
Whe' all meh wahbeen does stay.

It was with some difficulty that I managed to give attention
to the beleaguered figure. Once more I said, "The state of
education in the country today is in disarray and in shambles.
The people who were once regarded for their high literacy are
now tottering; and I remind you of your continued speech in
1961, *How can we hope to develop a modern, prosperous and*

happy society unless our people are well educated and well trained in the modern technological skills? The new education system which the People's National Congress will establish will be relevant to our experience, environment and needs, and not a continuation of the old one, large parts of which are irrelevant and meant for a subject people.[1]

"Today, the educational system thrust on the Guyanese by you and the People's National Congress leaves them exposed to further retrogression. Sure, you introduced free education, but to learn what? It was not long after you took over the schools that textbooks and school materials became scarce. In the field of education Guyana failed to keep abreast with the rest of the world and thus became a land which time forgot. Yet in 1960 any student from Queen's and other schools could match wits with any other student of the same age in any part of the world to show how capable the children of Guyana were. Today, extra tutoring after school hours is the order of the day if a student is to get ahead. Unheard of in my day! This is the age of information and computer technology but the children of Guyana are not aware of what is happening in the world. They are so far behind and it will be a Herculean task to bring them forward quick enough to meet the challenges that lie ahead. Education should have been one of your chief priorities since the greatest asset was the people. Our natural resources could not be developed without the efforts of the people and they needed to be educated and trained."

Meanwhile proceedings were moving along in the auditorium. Laudatory remarks were being uttered to those alumni who had made an effort to be present for the celebrations. It was amazing that I could hear and see what was taking place on stage and still be visiting the front hall of Hades. I was thinking that I could go on addressing Burnham on the school and the educational theme, but I needed to delve into other matters. I had to utilise my time. There was so

---

[1] p.10

much to discuss! I do not know if the Brickdam building was satisfied with my statements. I said to the encumbered figure, "By your actions you have deprived the students of Queen's a proper education. Like the votes of the people, you stole from those children their opportunity to give their best. It is a deed not worthy of a man whose fortunes were based on the education received at Queen's. I will depart from this topic but before I do so I would like to read to you a poem that I wrote in 1986. Although it was after your earthly death you are held responsible since degraded circumstances do not occur instantly but over a period of time. In your case degradation came in a short time. I have entitled this poem 'The Old School Yard'. These verses would not bring you relief but they do summarise the reasons for the poor state of education:

So many yesterdays have passed,
Yet I remember playing in the school yard.
It was wonderful those schoolboy days:
Laughter, fun, games, friendship, serious study.
There was no want for books, and pens, and paper;
No lack of food, nor drink, nor water.

I've passed the old school yard more recently.
I could scarcely believe my eyes,
The building needs repair and also a coat of paint.
There is no school yard now but a junk pile.
I am told that books, and pens, and paper
Are very difficult items to acquire.

What has happened here I asked myself.
The war had ended when I was here,
And peace has been with us for over forty years.
In fact after I had left here things got better
As I headed for another Alma Mater.
Why this neglect? I venture further
To hear it's not only here, but everywhere.

What are you telling me?
That under my British master I fared better?
You mean to say this fight for freedom
To be on my own was all in vain?
We fought so hard for our independence,
And I thought it would be to build
More schools, more school yards, more everything!

You mean to say that no one understands,
That it all starts here in the school yard?
Those little ones who run, jump and play
Eventually become the masters of the day,
But unless they are taught and shown
Surely they will pass unknown.
No books, no pens, no paper!
Soon I'll hear, "No competent teachers either".

I must protest to the competent authority,
This independence has not served us well.
If this situation continues to persist
Only morons here will dwell.
There must be books, and pens and paper,
Food, drink and refreshing water.
Life is shorter than a candle's burn
And in the school yard is where a child must learn.

The wooden building moved and the figure winced once more.

Casting my eyes downwards from the building I encountered the metal noose and this to my mind was the most serious encumbrance on Burnham's bodiless apparition. The label 'DISENFRANCHISE' told the tale. I continued to speak to the phantom, "The elections held in December 1964 were the last free and fair elections prior to October 1992. During the ensuing years all general elections and the referendum on the constitution were rigged. The population make-up of Guyana placed the East Indians as the majority and the Negro population as second. In a numbers game there was no way that your party could have won a majority of seats and thus retained power. To combat this dismal future you resolved to overseas voting to boost the electoral lists. The Government was in charge of the lists and therefore had control. Without any remorse you manipulated the voting system so that the eventual result in the 1968 election was an overall majority for the governing PNC, the party of which you were the leader.

"Democracy took flight far in advance of the spacecraft that took the astronauts to the moon. The successful exercises of fraud bolstered your confidence and steeled your criminal mind. World opinion did nothing and this successful violation of the democratic rights of the Guyanese people was a forerunner to more wicked contemplations."

The compiled speeches in *A Destiny to Mould* fail to shed any light on the post-victory motives of Burnham in the 1968 elections. In a speech quoted earlier and made on 27th March 1961 it was Burnham who said, *The People's National Congress believes in the democratic freedoms as embodied in the charter of Human Rights. It will establish these rights and freedoms, many of which have never been in existence in Guyana before. It will protect them.*

The PNC believes that there should always be free elections, freedom of speech, freedom of worship and the other freedoms, and much more important freedom from hunger and the freedom to work.[1]

Looking at the events after the 1968 election, I can only say that the PNC was free to cast the votes of the people. Let those who themselves know recall how and when they turned up to vote they were told that they had already voted. Then there was the case of the investigations of places of residence of those on the overseas lists only to find that the voters were horses and cattle in many fields. The events and circumstances reminded

---

[1] p.12

me of what I read in a book. It was cited by another author but it was so much to the point. It read, *Even the dead could be called upon: on one occasion a whole cemetery, seven hundred strong, gave their vote, and it was edifying to see that though they had been illiterate in their lifetime, they had all learned to write in the grave.*[c] · All I can say is that the ballots cast were very well protected as they changed places. The speech did not end with those freedoms and the protection offered seemed to me to be the type offered by the gangster Al Capone in Chicago in the United States of America during the days of prohibition. The speech further stated, *The People's National Congress is the party of Guyana and I invite you to rally under the banner of the PNC, the party of the new nation, to end the frustration which we have experienced so far, to join in the task in developing Guyana now, and to help in building a new society, a free society, and independent society, a society where political and social democracy will be established by the People's National Congress.*[1]

Without being too unkind I can only say that the only society that Burnham built and left standing was an ailing one, so much so that it was close to being a burial society. Freedom and democracy went on extended vacations. Corruption, incompetence, inefficiency, ineptitude, discrimination and fear took root and flourished, fertilised by the PNC's policies.

Once more I was drawn to calypso music. The saxophone accompanist was taking hold of me as he went into a short solo. The king of Caribbean song continued:

A woman walk in a store on Main Street.
Slippers on she feet, dutty petticoat, long time straw hat
And she smelling worse than that.
But she walk out like a lady,

---

[c] Gerald Brenan, *The Spanish Labyrinth*, cited by C.A. Yansen in his book, *Random Remarks on Creolese*, p.168.
[1] p.13

High heels, glasses, jewellery!
The straw hat she had on wearing before
She take match and she burn it inside the store.

I don't care if the whole ah BG burn down.
I ain't care if all ah Bookers burn down!
But they'll be putting me out me way
If they tackle Tiger Bay
And burn down me hotel
Whe' all meh wahbeen does stay.

What is sweetness to some is bitterness to others and I could observe there was no joy on Burnham's face as the music played on.

I spoke once more, "The protection offered was clearly to ensure that the PNC remained in office. The Guyanese people were not given a chance to express their will and the seizure of the government by those dastardly acts only assisted in widening the cleavage of the two main racial groups in the society. In your radio broadcast of 19th December, 1964, you said: *Our government does not consider, despite the unfortunate happenings of the past seven years, that there is in this country any deep-seated antipathy between the races, but recognises that our misfortunes have stemmed from the evil machinations of those bent upon the establishment of a totalitarian dictatorship founded on hatred, violence and a mutual distrust.*

...We know the world is looking at us. Some of the cynical pessimists are waiting to say, 'I told you so'. We intend to confound our critics and to prove that in the realm of human relations we can teach the world and make a name, 'to point a moral and adorn a tale.[1] Those were your words and after your actions in 1968 I would say emphatically that if there were no deep-seated antipathy between the races then your felonious seizure of the ballots of the people heralded that antipathy. You

---

[1] p.45

spoke of those bent on totalitarian dictatorship and today history records that you were Guyana's first and only dictator. Needless to say, it came to light that there was no morality in your actions and the tale that has to be told cannot adorn anything but extol the passiveness of the Guyanese people. Cast your memory back to 1981 when you were in London and had the hall of the expensive Grosvenor House Hotel in Park Lane hired for your address to the Guyanese living there; and remember how Scotland Yard had to whisk you and your wife away after someone in the crowd shouted, 'Dictator!' The meeting broke up and the money paid for the hall was forfeited."

The figure winced as I was not only touching certain nerves but pinching them. I did not call for help but the legendary Sparrow continued on:

They send for soldiers quite up in England
With big confusion.
They bring down warships with cannon like peas
To shoot Guyanese.
But BURNHAM say, "Alright now,
I am the only man could stop this row."
He give we the signal and that's the case.
Now we have peace and quiet in the place.

But I ain't care if the whole ah BG burn down!
I ain't care if all ah Bookers burn down!
They'll be putting me out me way
If they tackle Tiger Bay
And burn down me hotel
Whe' all meh wahbeen does stay.

Knowing that Burnham was familiar with the calypso I watched his face as Sparrow called his name. It was as if, apart from being stabbed, the knife was being turned. Burnham was in utter agony now and I gathered that this state would be repetitive since the music would be continuous. He had banned the calypso because his name was mentioned and now it would never stop playing.

I chimed in with a quote from the book, citing extracts from a speech delivered at the People's National Congress annual congress held in Georgetown on 5th November, 1961: *The People's National Congress controls the city, the People's National Congress controls the heart of the country, the People's National Congress as the election results have shown, also controls all the organised and industrialised area of Guiana...*[1] Those were your words and the Sparrow had said, "I am the only man could stop this row" and with this I concur since when the leader speaks the group often listens. I could not help but recall the question asked by Mr Gebrie-Egzy of Ethiopia when you addressed the United Nations Special Committee of Twenty-Four at the United Nations in New York on March 8th, 1963.

Mr Gebrie-Egzy (Ethiopia): *I should like to ask, as I did the other time last year of the Prime Minister of British Guiana, a question about the last disturbance which took place in British Guiana. In that disturbance some people said that the police and the civil service people did not discharge their duties properly. Or if it was not said openly, there was some insinuation that they did not do their duty properly. Since you are a member of the Opposition, I am sure that you would be able to tell us what the situation was from your point of view.*[2] Your answer to the question was partially true in that the report of the Commission of Enquiry stated that the police carried out their duties well and loyally but you dared not tell the gentleman that you controlled the city that had suffered severe damage. What I do know is that you had so much control that on many occasions you escorted my brother Fenton, who was the Attorney General during those troubled times, safely home.

---

[1] p.17
[2] p.91

Meanwhile, proceedings in the auditorium continued. A presentation of the Queen's College 'Book of Records' was being made to the President of Guyana by the author Dr Laurence Clarke. An error had actually been made before this when it was thought that the President would be making the feature presentation at this time. The President was surprised as it was premature. Matters were rectified and the ceremony proceeded as planned.

Chapter Five

Down in this gloomy sector of Avernus, I wanted to continue on the voting and election issues. I reminded Burnham of excerpts of the speech he made on winning the 1968 General Election when he addressed the masses at Independence Square on 22nd December, 1968, *Comrades and Friends, tonight as I stand before you I am deeply grateful for the way in which you by your votes have responded to the call of the PNC for a clear majority in the election just past.*

The success which the efforts of the PNC and you have achieved is a victory for the Guyanese people and for Guyana. I thank you both for your support and for the calm and restrained manner in which you conducted yourself during the trying period when all manner of abuse and provocation was directed at you. You have shown the world that the Guyanese electorate is a mature and sophisticated one. Your behaviour has surprised our detractors and has disappointed those who came to scoff.[1] As I read the passage I could not help but think how foolish the man was to think that he was convincing the people of Guyana and the world that he had won an honest and fair election. Fooling himself all the way and laying the foundation for imprisoning the people of Guyana and depriving them of their just rights. In that same speech he continued, *The result of the poll has shown that contrary to expectations of the bigots and the shortsighted, we have crossed racial frontiers in a significant manner. We have breached the PPP stronghold in the Corentyne and elsewhere. This is of importance to us as*

---

[1] p.59

a party but it is of even more importance to the Guyanese nation. It is the most significant development of the election. For now we know that the PPP knows and the world knows that Guyanese, regardless of their ethnic origin, are not the property of any one political party; that the majority of Guyanese are interested in the welfare of the nation as a whole rather than in the narrow interest of a part of the nation.

The support which we have received from all races and classes in Guyana compels recognition that, whatever label was put on us before, we are now recognised as the truly nationalist party which we have always claimed to be, and can speak for, and are responsible to, all the people of Guyana.[1] I imagined the scene at the delivery of the speech and thought how bold the counterfeiter was to think that he was convincing people and the world that he had bridged the wide election gap between the two major races. I spoke out, "Did you really believe that the world and the Guyanese people were convinced that you had won the election fair and square? By stealing those people's votes you did make them the property of the PNC. Remember what you said on 18th November, 1962, at Parade Ground, Georgetown, when addressing an open-air meeting and when you were insistent on having proportional representation: ...*As we pointed out before we left, proportional representation was not a political gambit or cheap gimmick for putting out the PPP and putting in the PNC. It was a solution which we had arrived at after careful thought. It would ensure that every political party got the number of seats to which it was entitled. It would ensure that cooperation between the political parties would then be compulsory, would then be obligatory rather than optional. It would mean that the general masses of the country would recognise that no political party could dominate the country or any other political parties...*[2] If you believed that no one party could dominate and that it would force a coalition, why did you

---

[1] p.60
[2] p.81

not choose this direction? Did you really believe that in four short years you would be able to win over voters of the *Opposition* to an extent that the PNC would have a majority in Parliament? This could never happen by a natural process. If the *Opposition* party was listening to your words they would have sensed that the next election of 1973 would find the PNC not only with a majority but with over a two-thirds majority. This would then give you the opportunity to force upon the people a constitution of your own. You would have a free hand and only Fate could have stopped you. I say this confidently because in the speech of 22nd December, 1968, your words were: *We hope that by our efforts the next election will find us with more support than we have at present.*[1] Like one who is gifted with prophetic powers already you had signalled the results of the next election having been successful with the villainous exercises of the 1968 election. It was not necessary to win political power, it could just be taken like taking candy from the mouths of babes. I say to you that Guyana was doomed. Larceny was given a high place and it would pervade the society, as you well know. Your future actions would show that all the people of Guyana would become the property of the People's National Congress since their casting of votes would be decided for them. The people no longer had a voice in their affairs."

Having made his presentation to President Jagan, Dr Clarke then presented his compilation of the 'Former Headmasters' Reports' to the Headmistress of the School. This was very generous of him since the compilation of these reports was not an easy task.

In my immediate situation I continued to hear the sweet calypso music of the Mighty Sparrow. Luckily for me, it was the only pleasant sound in this dismal place. 'BG War' was supplying fuel for my continuing encounter with Burnham. I found that I needed to reproach the tortured apparition once

---

[1] p.60

more. I cautioned him with excerpts from his address to the United Nations Special Committee of Twenty-Four on 8th March, 1963, at the United Nations.

The representative from the United States spoke; Mr Blake (United States): *I should like to ask the petitioner for perhaps two points of clarification here. In most democratic countries in the world it is not found particularly necessary to have a system as complicated as the one of proportional representation. I wonder if there is any particular or special justification why that should be done in British Guiana and whether this is likely to delay independence.*

I should like to ask the petitioner for some clarification on the question of racial organisation among the parties. We have heard on this committee before that this was the case. Does the petitioner feel that it is a system that will work for the welfare of the people of British Guiana?

Mr Burnham: *The proposal for proportional representation which the People's National Congress advocates is not a complicated system. The proposal is to have the entire country as one constituency and the voters being permitted to vote for the party of their choice, and then the parties being allocated seats in direct proportion to the number of popular votes polled. We do not accept the suggestion either that in the majority of democratic countries this system of proportional representation, or some variation of it, is not to be found. It exists in Tasmania, it exists in Scandinavian countries, it exists in a number of the Latin American countries also. In our case, we have found it necessary to propose this system of proportional representation.*

I did not want to raise this because it struck me as being primarily a domestic matter because we are convinced that if the opportunity were given to one party, the party in office at the moment, it would get an overwhelming majority of seats on a minority of votes. There is reason to believe that it would seek to establish an authoritarian regime through the legislative process. But with proportional representation, in the foreseeable future that is an impossibility and an overall majority of seats would express an overall majority support throughout the country.

The representative of the United States asked about racial loyalties so far as the political parties are concerned. It is true that in the 1961 elections the greater part of the voting was along racial lines. The majority of the Indians voted for the People's Progressive Party, the majority of Africans voted for the People's National Congress and the majority of Portuguese and mixed peoples voted for the United Force.

It is our opinion in the People's National Congress that that is most undesirable, and that voters should be led to support a party on the basis of programme and capacity rather than on the ethnic origin of the respective leaders. It is further our opinion that if proportional representation, such as we propose, were to be instituted in Guyana, that would assist in the lessening of racial voting or, as we put it, in hurdling the racial obstacle because no party under proportional representation can possibly in the foreseeable future get an overall majority of seats if it merely appealed to race. If, however, any party under proportional representation really desired and worked for an overall majority of seats, it would have to cross the ethnic barrier and lessen this racial voting. That is our opinion.[1]

"That was a very nice speech made before a specific group. You spoke of the country being one constituency and that seats were to be allotted in proportion to the votes received. The voters would vote for the party of their choice and the parties would be allocated seats proportionally. Yet after the 1964 election you persuaded people from the Opposition to cross the floor and join your party when those very people were nominated by the opposing party, and thus they did not have free will to cross the floor but had to be replaced if they decided to leave the opposition parties. Have you forgotten that you asked Fenton to be the Attorney General in the Coalition

[1] p.91

Government? He had to turn you down on a question of principle as he was a member of the PPP. You then went in search of Mr Sonny Ramphal. The floor crossing suited your purpose as it eventually led to the PNC having a majority through devious means. The PNC really worked for an overall majority as it worked on members of its coalition partner, the United Force. Tell me which party ended up being authoritarian?

"You spoke of other countries having proportional representation and this is so but those countries are content to have coalition governments and there is no effort on one party conniving to cheat other parties through vote rigging. The people's welfare is more of their concern than the quest for power and domination. That is the difference. Coalition governments in those countries are concerned with seeing the development and progress of the state so as to ensure that the people who are governed benefit and are not put at a disadvantage.

"On two occasions you mentioned that it would be an impossibility in the foreseeable future for any one party to have a majority of seats under proportional representation. Yet in 1968, four years after being in power, a majority was achieved and all the world knows that it was through fraud and rigging. As you proclaimed your counterfeit victory to the crowd the birth of Guyana's first authoritarian regime was taking place.

"Simultaneously, rigor mortis was setting in on democracy and a massacre of the people's rights had commenced. In retrospect you cannot deny the truth of these comments. In your address to the UN Committee of Twenty-Four you managed very well to fool them all. They had no inkling of Guyana's fate. The Opposition was to establish an authoritarian regime is what you said but you are remembered as a dictator of the first class. A mouldy destiny was being forged for the Guyanese people that would lead them to a life of drudgery and a constant barrage of humiliation by other peoples of the Caribbean. The mould of the nation that you were creating was not dissimilar to the moulding of jello pudding – soft and firm in a cold environment but turning to liquid and then evaporating in the tropical heat. The foundation for nationhood was not only soft but also porous so that in the final analysis a nation that would be strong and proud could never come into being because of its crumbling base. Having seized power and not winning it you had no commitment to civil liberties. Like a bulldozer you mowed down all obstacles.

"The reluctance of the disenfranchised victims to retaliate with force was not surprising since they opted for peace and they did not want to engage in violence and destruction despite the forfeiture of their most precious rights. They had been exposed to violence and disturbances when you were in the Opposition, and now that you held power and were supported by the army, the police and other forces, it would have been futile to offer resistance. In that same speech of 22nd December, 1968, at Independence Square you said, *We do not deny the right of the opposition to oppose but as a government we will not permit the destruction of our national life in any manner. We are equipped materially and psychologically to deal firmly, impartially and swiftly with all who by any means or any guise may be so ill-advised as to seek to spoil our record of peace and tranquillity to gratify their puerile ambitions.*[1] You cannot say that during your tenure of office as head of the Government that you have ever experienced any disturbances as happened during the early sixties before you came into power. This is not surprising since you were now wearing the other shoe and I could not see you erupting against yourself. I often told friends how noticeably the violence had disappeared after you came to power. I have always felt that you would have served Guyana best by being the leader of the Opposition since you controlled so many facets of the society. Cheddi could not have done anything drastic and get away. You would have called out your dogs."

---

[1] p.61

The calypso legend was experiencing competition from above as the Guyana Police Force was entertaining the audience during an interlude. Good as they were, my ears were really fine-tuned to the saxophone playing in calypso. The competition was merely physical as my heart and soul were with the calypso king.

Chapter Six

I decided to shift the topic and broach the subject of the thing that looked like a dentist's chair around his left arm. This was a most interesting object with a very sad story behind it. I found that I was not addressing him by any name and I wanted to change this. Coming from Queen's it was not difficult to find an appropriate name for him. In the Upperworld he was known as 'Odo' and the 'Kabaka'. I always had a name for him and now I decided that it was time I used it. It was an appropriate name and suited him. My name for him was 'Banjoboy', indeed no Guyanese could realistically claim that Burnham was not the architect of banning in modern times. It reminded me of those gods in mythology who would ban someone to a deserted island; the only difference was that Burnham's was real, even the 'god' part. When I attended horse-races at Durban Park there was a horse by the name of Banjo Boy. I forgot the name of the owner but it does not really matter because Banjo Boy was never any good. He could not compare with horses like Dancing Master, the little filly Rockfell, Pensive, Ulupi, Havoc, Waverly and Churchgrass. Horse-racing fans can tell you about those horses. Banjo Boy was not top class in his domain but 'Banjoboy' was a champion. He banned from left to right so much so that he banned the use of the Guyana dollar outside of Guyana. The money was useless in the Caribbean and Guyana was a member of Caricom. I do not know if butterflies were banned from Georgetown or if they stayed away of their own accord but they were markedly absent when I made visits to Guyana. Butterflies flourish in an environment where there are plenty of bright flowers. The state of the people's gardens were no longer attractive because of neglect. Who had time and energy for gardens when life was becoming difficult? The butterflies must have found more congenial places. What I liked about Banjoboy was that he banned the importation of Scotch whisky but he would put the Chivas Regal in a rum bottle and tell the crowd that he only drank rum. I knew that when he had a drink at the Woodbine Hotel it was not rum! On one occasion he even told his hostess on a visit to her home that he only used rum in fruitcake! I was very upset when he banned the Sparrow's 'BG War'. People will tell you that Sparrow is my number one favourite. And why is this?

To most peoples of the world, the Caribbean islands are known for their beautiful beaches, blue waters and lovely sunshine. Tropical sunsets and evenings caressed by gentle winds set the scene for amorous and romantic adventures. These islands are linked by the common sharing of the Atlantic Ocean and the Caribbean Sea, and by the common heritage of culture and development. Scattered and separated, they are jewels in the sea, each island displaying a characteristic of its own. Yet these islands have become bonded by one man whose contribution to the Caribbean makes him a legendary genius. This genius is Slinger Francisco, better known as the Mighty Sparrow in Caribbean circles and to those people of the Caribbean who have migrated to other parts of the world.

Slinger Francisco was born in Grenada but lived most of his life in Trinidad and Tobago. As a singer of calypso – the West Indian folk song – the Mighty Sparrow has set himself aloft from other calypso singers. His first album in 1957 was electrifying and full of excitement and it set the foundation for greater achievements. Sparrow's calypsos are his own compositions and are often in tune with current events, both domestic and international. Also known as Birdie, Sparrow is an international performer of renown. His showmanship, his brilliance and his musical talent have made him the calypso king of the world.

Sparrow's calypsos have covered various topics and the accompanying music to the lyrics has always been infectious. Through his songs and vibrant energy he has linked up the Caribbean, and when West Indians, no matter where they are, hear him singing, they cannot help but be affected. Cricket has done a similar thing for the West Indies but the Sparrow has edged it out of the position of chief binder. Sparrow has dominated the calypso world and when the day comes when he no longer will sing for us the end of an era would have been precipitated. As West Indians we should consider ourselves fortunate to have in our midsts this man who, in performing his art, has left a legacy so rich that were he of another place he would be remembered as the world remembers Irving Berlin, Jerome Kern, William Shakespeare, Robert Frost, Nat 'King' Cole, Frank Sinatra, to name only a few. Sparrow's genius was used to bond and unite in contrast to Burnham whose every move was divisive. 'BG War' was being played in the background as a constant reminder to Burnham whose favourite calypso was 'Archie Bruk Dem Up'.

I addressed the apparition, "Banjoboy, and you are aware of why I call you this. As an old QC boy, you should not be surprised. You can take teasing although in this environment it is difficult since you are under a tremendous strain." The apparition moved a little but this only caused some more discomfort. I am sure that I triggered his memory into remembering some of the items and foods which he banned under the pretence of saving foreign currency when in fact it was poor financial management and lack of fiscal restraint resulting in failure to satisfy creditors. One of the main items that was banned was wheaten flour. The replacement for wheaten flour was to be rice flour. But what can replace wheaten flour after one has been accustomed to bread and roti since childhood? But if rice flour or any other type of flour could have made bread similar to the type made from wheat then I am of the opinion that bread as we know it in Guyana would not have been in existence.

"Our society has developed from the arrival of immigrants from Africa, China, Portugal, Holland and India, and I am sure they would have brought that formula for making bread and roti from rice flour if it ever existed. And what of food for the infants and small children? Baby food was banned and educated though you were you seemed not to have known that the feeding of infants and small children from birth to about the age of five or six years is most important in that time of their lives. Those formative years had to be supported with adequate and nourishing food or else their grounding would be hollow for the future. The destiny of the children's lives was being moulded and there was no way that it could be changed. The banning of basic foods led to malnutrition and the development of 'white corner' mouths. The banning of baby foods was a criminal act as adequate substitutes were not developed.

"Guyanese culture had as its base products like white-eye – a kind of bun, butterflap, sweet-bread, tennis-roll, collar, pine-tart, patties, duff, dumpling, coconut biscuits and other delicious pastries and cakes which all depended on the availability of flour. How sweet it was to enjoy a bara and potato-ball before taking a seat in the cinema! Just as enjoyable was a large mauby with ice coupled with a white-eye or tennis-roll. One of the many segments of Guyanese culture was eliminated with the ban of flour. Let me remind you of what you said on May 26th, 1969, ...*that though in the distant past our forbears came from many lands, with varied and varying cultures, we, who are born here, share a common heritage, and that today the ties that bind us are faster and more numerous than the differences which would keep us apart. Today in Guyana, it is heartening to note a new awareness of the value of our diversity and respect for, and acceptance of, the customs and cultures of the peoples who comprise our country – customs and cultures out of which we can create richer ones uniquely*

Guyanese.[1] Did you not think that the kind of foods we ate and which we liked were part of our culture? And do you think it is easy to develop new tastes? It is over thirty years since I ate a bara at the Empire Cinema, but I can still taste it. For the East Indian community the banning of split peas along with the ban on flour was more serious for them than for other ethnic groups as it meant that the traditional dholl (similar in some way to French Canadian pea soup), and dhollpouri, described by the one time Governor of British Guiana, Sir Alfred Savage, as "the pancake with the peas inside", were no longer readily available. These and rice were their staples. I say they were not readily available since the two items of flour and split peas were available to some as smuggling soon commenced in Guyana. Given that the staples of flour and split peas were now banned you boasted to the world, despite these deprivations and unpopular measures, that the Indian community supported your party at election time to ensure that the PNC remained in power. If there were no reasons to vote against you, surely you now gave them the best reason since you were attacking their stomachs and breeding their disdain? The workers in the rice and sugar industries, those in the bauxite industry who mined the bowels of the earth and faced the torrid heat of the calcining furnaces, and those in other places toiled very hard. To grant them these simple, essential items would never have counterbalanced their arduous labours.

"As a result of your banning flour and other items, coupled with the flow of emigration, certain skills started to disappear, so that the country was losing part of its cultural heritage. What was happening is expressed in a poem that I composed, and you cannot disagree with its contents. I have titled this poem 'Lost Skills':

I asked a question about a wooden vat
Because it would have served to fit the bill.

---

[1] p.149

The answer given was, 'That is true'. But
Can you believe that throughout the land
Only one remains who has got the skill?

'Nuttin! Nuttin! Get your nuttin here!',
A familiar sound of yesteryear.
No more to be heard, no nuttin anywhere.
No one can make this candy anymore;
No ingredients, the skills no longer there.

Tennis-roll! Tennis-roll! Mauby and tennis-roll!
Flour and water transformed to a heart's desire.
One cannot see a tennis-roll in any place,
Not home, not in the shops, or market-place.
No ingredients or skills for one to trace.

Fish and bread, whenever the train had stopped.
No more train, no more fish and bread to buy.
The skills are there, but the larder is just bare.
No flour, no yeast, good oil you cannot buy.
But most of all, the train line is no longer there.

Butterscotch candy! Remember this tasty one!
Who can make this wonderful candy now?
Gone! Far gone! The skills for making this one
And many, many others have disappeared also.
The skills are lost, the skills have gone.

"It was you who, on 26th May, 1969, addressing a mass meeting at the Queen Elizabeth II National Park in Georgetown on the occasion of the third anniversary of independence, said, *...We now mill our own flour at a cheaper price to the consumer than that of imported flour...*[1] On achieving absolute power, flour, whether locally produced or imported, became a banned item. You set out to prove that man does not live by

---

[1] p.147

bread alone! Under your instructions the police were told to seize bread from vendors and, as if that were not enough, they were told to trample upon the bread! No longer was there the joy of smelling that sweet aroma emitted from the baking of bread whether at home or in the bakeries. At many festivities items made from wheaten flour were seized and confiscated. It was considered an offence to have banned items in your possession. You, a President for life, found satisfaction in taking away the simple pleasures of life from the people. As mentioned before, the consequence of banning was the development of rampant smuggling and other despicable acts. In some instances women granted to men, especially sailors, who came into the ports of Guyana, favours for items such as flour, onions, garlic, cooking oil and other types of household necessities. Anything to assist in the feeding of their families. Integrity and morality were on Death Row. It would appear that you were ignorant of the fact that onions and garlic besides giving flavour to foods had medicinal value. You just banned for banning sake, Banjoboy! Items such as apples, grapes and pears, which were Christmas favourites and which I grew up with as a child, were also banned. The last shipments of apples to reach Guyana were destroyed and buried by Customs' officials. They were not given away, as that would have been penalty enough, but returned to the good earth which had nurtured and presented them for ultimate consumption in the Upperworld. It is difficult to query the principle of self-reliance but what must one do when there are no substitutes to rely on. Where were the local replacements and how often were they available? I tell you now that changing the tastes of grown people is perhaps the most difficult thing to do, if not impossible. Recall your last request before going to the Georgetown Hospital for the operation on your throat! It was for sweetened condensed milk, which was a banned item, but which was readily available in your own household. You felt no shame in asking! I imagine that nectar of milk tasted sweeter than usual!

"The banning of tinned items such as corned beef and sardines created hardship for those people who had to go into the interior to work. Fresh meat and fish were not always available because there were times when game and fish were difficult to acquire. The tinned foods assisted enormously. I speak from firsthand experience having worked for three-month periods in the interior prior to taking up studies abroad. For those who did not have to go into the interior the banning of those two items put a halt to a quick snack or meal.

"Many food and consumer goods were banned from importation including the importation of cooking oil. Guyanese were told that they must use local coconut oil despite the knowledge that it was high in cholesterol and thus detrimental to one's health. However, what was disturbing and offensive was that you would have the Consulate of Guyana in New York fly out with the help of Guyana Airways gallons of no cholesterol sunflower oil for your own household. You and members of your family's health would escape exposure to the ravages of cholesterol." A.G. came to mind again, *Jayme, this is what 'im say, but man this is what 'im do.*

Early in his tenure of office, Burnham banned the importation of the American magazine *Ebony* since in one of its publications there was an article indicating that he had become the fifth richest black man in the world. The general ban now included books and magazines. However, Burnham received the latest in reading matter from overseas. The bookshops of Guyana were now depleted of suitable reading material. The place which was once so modern with information of events all over the world was now thrown into the abyss of ignorance. The people were being slowly deprived of contact with the outside world, all in the game plan to make them backward and totally dependent on the few PNC 'wise' men. Nothing was withheld from the Burnham household as I overheard on many occasions in the Consulate of Guyana, conversations in which someone would say, "And I am sending Vi's things as requested", Vi being Burnham's wife. Payment for the items sent must have been from the taxpayers' accounts since access to foreign funds and the exporting of it was a criminal offence. This hypocrisy was allowed to go on until Burnham's earthly death in 1985. However, let us leave the banning for a while and examine the story behind the dentist's chair.

Burnham invited at regular intervals an American female dentist to Guyana for her to give dental treatment to himself and members of the PNC hierarchy. All dental work was done at the expense of the Guyanese taxpayers and only top PNC members were privileged to this perquisite. In 1979 one of Burnham's ministers, Vincent Teekah, was being treated late by the dentist whose workplace was situated in Thomas Lands adjacent to Vlissengen Road. Teekah was once a member of the PPP and having been absent from political life for a short while returned, quitting the PPP and joining the PNC. Burnham appointed him a Government minister. It was felt in some PNC circles that Teekah was getting too close to Burnham and even becoming a favourite. Teekah was an Indian and his becoming a favourite of Burnham was not going down well with certain members of the PNC. There were reports also that Burnham may have been considering appointing him Prime Minister as a constitutional decoration giving credence to the vote rigging exercises.

Teekah had an appointment in October 1979 with the lady dentist and as he lay reclined in the dentist's chair a gunman entered the dentist's surgery and shot him somewhere in the region of the groin. The bullet hit this area because he was trying to get out of the chair when faced by the gunman. The bullet was meant to hit him in the heart. Teekah was not killed instantly. He begged for his life as instant surgery would have saved him but his calls went unheeded. He was removed from the dentist's premises and taken by car to a place close to the location of Banks Brewery which was close to the Demerara River. This place would be at a diagonal to the dentist's office and was over a mile away. He was left there bleeding until death took him. There must have been some premeditation in this incident since it was quite obvious that Teekah would be helpless in the dentist's chair. Teekah died and was buried. Burnham was not responsible for his death but the public perception was that a member of the party and a minister of Government were its perpetrators. To this day an inquest has never been held although it has been said that Burnham was very upset and vowed that he would find the parties involved. They were never found. The lady dentist was whisked out of the country and I believe never came back to do any more dental work.

I accosted the apparition, "Banjoboy, I want to remind you of Vincent Teekah. Have you noticed that he is not in this section of the halls of Hades? He was not tainted enough to find himself detained here. Also, he had a proper burial and his body has been lodged in a proper place. I understand that you were very upset at Teekah's assassination and you swore to get even. But you never did anything, never even held a small investigation. Having total control of the country and of its institutions, you could have done something! You were fully aware of the forces behind the killing but you could not do anything since you yourself may have come under threat of death by some foul means. Your best course was to let time pass and time, that great healer, would allow the matter to be forgotten. However, you can see that although it may have been forgotten in the Upperworld the authorities in Hades have not forgotten and the weighty chair now adorns your person. I remind you again of your speech of 1st March, 1962, in the Legislative Assembly, *So far as I am aware, a plot to assassinate or kill any person is still a criminal offence punishable under Chapter 10 of the Laws of British Guiana.*[1] That section of the law of Guyana has not been repealed nor replaced as far as I know. When you made that speech you were in the Opposition. When Teekah was assassinated you were the big chief or shall I say Kabaka, and any directive

---

[1] p.27

given by you would have been carried out. You certainly could have called back the lady dentist or got a statement from her. But the Guyanese people were not entitled to an explanation and Teekah's family less so. The people were like sheep grazing on a green and you the shepherd could lead them anywhere and do anything. They never objected nor gave any indication that they ever would. Guyanese society had become complacent and would absorb all the shocks presented to it. You often spoke a great deal about performance but whenever it was really needed you failed miserably."

This confrontation made the figure uncomfortable and he fidgeted. However, any time he made the slightest move the barbed wire would inflict pain. I was certain that my visit was most unwelcome but I needed to go on for the sake of the children and people of Guyana and also myself. I could not deprive history of this record. Other writers have perhaps gone into Burnham's politics and political ideology, dialectics and different things, but fair comment on the contents of *A Destiny to Mould* has never been made. In fact, I saw a headline in the 'Letters to the Editor' section of the *Stabroek News* edition of Tuesday September 27th, 1994, saying, "Burnham deserves a fair trial". The author in the article was saying that Burnham "...stood out, among the rest, as a man with charisma (a commanding, eloquent speaker), and a pragmatic visionary in Guyanese and West Indian affairs – Reference: his *a destiny to Mould.*" I have mentioned earlier the charisma and eloquence of Burnham but the visions of Burnham as recorded in the book never came close to actual achievement and many of the things he said he would do were never done especially in the areas of freedom and democracy. He would talk but he never performed. When I saw that headline soon after starting on this book it became most imperative that I achieved its completion. It was important for me to tell the story of the chameleon. I was making that attempt after my visit to Avernus.

I now wanted to cast his memory back to 1962 when there was a general strike resulting in riots and disturbances, as an objection to the Kaldor Budget of the PPP Government, and during which Superintendent Derek McLeod was shot and killed. Once again I had to go back to his speech in the Legislative Assembly on 1st March, 1962, when he said, *Mr Speaker, I am aware of the fact that since the hon. the Premier has informed this House that a Commission of Enquiry will be appointed to enquire into the incidents which occurred on Friday, 16th February, it would not be advisable in this discussion which the House has given me leave to initiate, to attempt to apportion any blame as to who was responsible for the incidents; for instance, who shot Superintendent McLeod and so on...*[1] I addressed the disembodied shade thus, "I have noticed the rifle with the name of 'McLEOD' adorning your person. I know that you did not pull the trigger of the rifle but I am putting it to you that it was upon your instructions that McLeod was shot. I am of the view that it was necessary that Englishman Superintendent McLeod be put away permanently since he was impartial and was only doing his duty as required of an officer of the police force. You are aware of this incident and your encumbrance confirms that you were knowledgeable although you told Parliament that you did not know who shot McLeod. The judges down here seem to know." In the background I could hear the Sparrow singing the last verse of 'BG War'.

"I remind you of the radio broadcast made on coming to power after the General Election of 1964 through a coalition with the United Force Party. This broadcast was made on 19th December, 1964, *This government is not bent on the confiscation of property; this government will not pursue policies likely to bring the races into collision; this government will maintain law and order; this government will see that the lives and property and personal safety of all citizens are protected.*[2] Words, beautiful words! Although there was no

---

[1] p.25
[2] p.45

uprising did you not believe that rigging of the votes was putting the races on a collision course? You created distrust and if ever you had a chance of winning over the Indians you now blew it. And what about those low prices paid for property that the Government acquired? With those low prices was it not the same as confiscation? Law and order, etc. etc.. What of Father Darke? I see an object like a spear marked 'DARKE'. Father Darke had to pay the ultimate sacrifice for Father Morrison. When the iron bar struck him in the back that fatal blow was meant for Father Morrison. Not knowing Father Morrison by sight the assailants thought that any white man dressed up like a priest and demonstrating was Father Morrison. So blindly, Father Darke was struck the fatal blow. Father Morrison was a thorn in your side as he stood up to the PNC with his editorials and articles in the small weekly publication, *Catholic Standard*. The suppression of the *Catholic Standard*'s articles was foremost as it was one of the few burning torches that stood alight in the darkness of your stewardship. Let me not forget to mention the small publication *Compass* which had its articles written and supported by some senior people in the nationalised organisations. Their lives were no longer comfortable. Any hint of criticism found disfavour with you. Those promised freedoms in your past speeches were like the post-independence election victories – all counterfeit. That broadcast of 19th December, 1964, sounds hollow to me but if it is not refuted it will read good in later years. In a speech on 14th April, 1963, you gave your definition of power, *Real power connotes the ability to govern effectively, to bring necessary changes to the social and economic systems, to weld various sections of Guiana into a nation, to put the country on the road to prosperity, to be accepted as the government, a government that performs and delivers.*[1] Once more I ask: Did you think that vote rigging would weld the various sections of Guyana and hence make a

---

[1] p.39

nation? Nations are built when there is trust and confidence and you could not command those. Was it necessary to ban flour, split peas, cooking oil, books, magazines, etc.; to change the social and economic systems? And how did your Government perform? And what did it deliver? I will tell you – a lowering of the standard of living of the Guyanese people, the emigration of disenchanted Guyanese, increased infant mortality, higher unemployment, a lower standard of education, a bankrupt Guyana in dire economic and financial straits, and immeasurable repression and fear."

As I was addressing Burnham, the chairman of the proceedings in the auditorium was making his introductory remarks pertaining to the guest speaker, His Excellency the President of Guyana, Dr Cheddi Jagan, whose presentation would be the feature address. I informed the apparition, "Banjoboy, Cheddi will be speaking shortly. I would like to inform you that he is now the President of Guyana after our first free and fair election since December 1964. I will tell you some more of that election later. If he says anything earth-shattering I will advise you although it would not help you in anyway. He could say that he was going to remove your symbolic body from the back of the Botanical Gardens and that would be good news for you and Guyana. I was told that if the symbolic body is not removed from there that you will remain in this posture for an unlimited time, almost forever. I do not think I am in a position to give advice down here but I think you should concentrate on appearing in someone's dream and asking them to remove the symbol, telling them at the same time that you are very uncomfortable and you do need relief."

Time was moving on but I was certain that the President's speech would not be a short one and I would have time to continue with my visit. I now wanted to address subjects like the Waterworks, the Electricity Corporation and the Post Office. I needed to know how to lead into the subjects through reference to the book. It was a bit difficult since there was no direct reference to these institutions. I came up with an ingenious idea that would have made my departed parents proud. Even my divine guardian would have given me high marks.

Kaieteur Fall

Brink of Kaieteur Fall

Orinduik Falls

Kaieteur Fall

Chapter Seven

It was well-known that the pure water supply of Georgetown, the capital, had deteriorated, but history records that the drinking water of Georgetown was regarded as one of the best in the world. Foreigners would rave about our drinking water and how wonderful the taste was as opposed to drinking water elsewhere which had the lingering taste of chemicals. Georgetown could really have boasted about her drinking water. It was crystal clear and truly tasty. Now I do not know if having clean, crystal clear drinking water is a European thing and, therefore, giving the people of Georgetown a different kind of water was getting them away from being Europeanised. This getting rid of European customs was very important to the Government, and the quicker the better. It was important to do away with all the trappings of the former masters. In a speech to the members of the People's National Congress at their Annual Congress in New Amsterdam on 14th April, 1963, Burnham said, ...*Robbed of all but the rudimentary aspects of their native culture they accepted European (English) social standards and norms, and set about being assimilated into a society dominated by the European. They seem to have placed great store on the acquiring of education and skills and though as a group they never reached the upper levels of the foreign society they were for practical purposes Europeanised.*[1] Burnham was speaking about the African slaves but his comments were pertinent to the whole population since they were all being ruled by the Europeans.

---

[1] p.40

The fact that this 'Europeanisation' had taken place hundreds of years ago and the descendants of the various peoples did not know anything more than what was being taught them did not seem to matter. That they would have developed a culture of their own in the process which would be Guyanese although it had extracts of European culture did not matter. The acquisition of education and skills were pro-European and these had to be de-emphasised hence the deterioration of the education system. This water business was foremost in my mind when he spoke of 'Europeanised' and I, having lived in Europe for some time, was of the view that I could give an accurate and true comment on the water issue.

I addressed the figure once more, "I imagine that you are thirsty in this place but there is no water around to quench your thirst. Do you remember the days before you became Prime Minister of British Guiana how the water in Georgetown was crystal clear and wonderful to drink? You are acquainted with what happened during your time Upstairs as head of the Government and how the water was no longer crystal clear but had a light brown tinge. It was supposed to be clean as far as bacteria went, but you must admit that when you have been accustomed to crystal clear water all of your life it is difficult to swallow water with a tinge. Do you remember how your Government was trying to speedily de-Europeanise the people? You know, like banning chocolates, biscuits, mackerel, whisky, vodka, paint and enamels, etc., etc.; books and magazines not being available; difficulties in getting paper and writing equipment and a host of other things. The list is so long. Well, I have news for you and I hope you can take it without flinching! When it comes to water the people are now re-Europeanised! The latest thing is bottled water. Yes, crystal clear water in a bottle. It is called 'Tropical Mist'. D'Aguiar's company is producing it and selling it in a twenty-six ounce bottle. You look so surprised! It is an absolute fact. I was having lunch one day at the Tower Hotel and I saw my glass being filled with crystal clear water from a bottle. I am not sure but I think it had a blue label. Of course I was taken back by this development. I thought I was in Italy or Spain or France or back in Belgium. When I thought of what you were trying to achieve I said to myself, like a true Guyanese, 'He ran from the coffin and butt up with the jumbie'. It reminded me of one of the Sparrow's calypsos, 'Smart Bajan', in which he sang about Trinidadians throwing coins in a fountain built by a Bajan engineer. This coin throwing was to bring good fortune after making a wish. This behaviour was mimicking the throwing of coins in the fountain in Rome, Italy. Sparrow said, 'Thousands of people were going up there daily, Trinidad was becoming just like Italy'. Guyana, however, had now joined the millions of bottled water drinkers. There was no doubt that social change was taking place. But do not look so surprised, for you can very well remember that you yourself were very much European when you dressed up in jodhpurs and rode on your horse, and do not forget the time when you dressed up in Davenport and tails to attend the funeral service on the death of Sir Winston Churchill.

"I cannot allow you to escape criticism for giving the Guyanese people cloudy stained glasses to drink out of. Do you remember that? Imagine, you traded our good bauxite and whatever else for those glasses as if you did not know that East Germany produced some of the finest crystal glassware in the world. Guyanese people had to drink out of those dirty-looking glasses. I know that you and yours never drank out of any of them. I could see a reason why you wanted to keep those glasses and did not complain or return them. They were very suitable when you consider that our water was not crystal clear any more and those cloudy holders would have done a good masking job. The more I think about it you really had contempt for the Guyanese people. I grew up in Guyana and cannot remember ever seeing glasses of that nature and to think that our top class bauxite was bartered for glasses that even the East Germans did not use. You took advantage of the people and they never did anything about it. On reflection I doubt whether they could have done anything."

Was I being too rough on him? Not in the least! This was an alumnus although his behaviour suggested that he did not want to be connected with the school. I found that the trouble with the PPP was that Cheddi, although he was an old QC boy, was no match for Burnham in cunning and smartness. I do not think that Cheddi wanted power as much as Burnham did. Whenever Guyana was to be given her independence, Burnham wanted to be sure that he was the man in charge. He wanted power to mould whatever he had in his mind. In the third anniversary speech on May 26th, 1969, Burnham had said, *...There are still too many of us who want to pattern our life on foreign standards, forgetting the Americans, the British, the Germans, the French, the Canadians, the Russians and others have in each case evolved their own cultures and set their own economic and social goals...*[1] Yet, he seemed to have forgotten that the Guyanese had developed a culture of their own and did have social and economic goals. The Guyanese after World War II were making every effort to see that their children were educated; that there was adequate and capable medical institutions to cater for the health of the nation; that development though slow was taking place, and they were doing everything that was necessary to build the society. Those who can remember may recall how our civil service was regarded as very competent and highly efficient. True, the heads of many institutions were non-Guyanese but the workforce was all Guyanese. Burnham's mouldy destiny was to destroy the civil service as we knew it and set up a service to his liking. The evolution that had taken place up to that time was to be discarded and the Burnham mould was to replace it.

I wanted to read to him in its entirety an article I had read in the *Catholic Standard,* a publication of the Catholic Church, and which Burnham found a menace to his maladministration. I

---

[1] p.149

spoke to the shackled shade, "I am going to read an article written by a top public servant in the June 3rd, 1990 edition of the *Catholic Standard* and which I have kept all this time. The heading is titled, 'Open Letter To Public Servants'. It reads as follows:

IT IS absurd for the Guyana Public Service Union to dismiss the WPA's statement to Senator Kennedy that public servants have been trained for political loyalty to the PNC as being 'irrational, unfounded and malicious' and that it showed 'great disrespect and utter disregard for public servants'.

In my thirty years as a public servant (both at ministries and public institutions) and one who held many positions in the Public Service Union going back to the 1960s, I am in a position to say that Mr Kwayana's statement, even though factual, does not even go far enough to show how employees in the public sector have been emasculated by the PNC over the years and made into docile tools of the ruling party.

In the 1960s we were instrumental in bringing down the PPP government by PNC dictated acts of sabotage leading to the 80 days strike. Talk about supporting the government of the day is mere theory. We were far from achieving this ideal when we were taught to work to rule, to pass out documents and information of the then PPP government to the PNC.

During the 80 days strike we were instructed to puncture the tyres of cars and bicycles of employees who refused to join the strike to render those employees immobile. Burnham and A.P. Alleyne met the leaders among us, often at party offices, and encouraged us on to even more dangerous, daring and nefarious activities in order to get 'de coolie government' out.

We were made to believe that the PNC was going to lead us to some Utopia, never believing that we were digging our own future economic graves.

Came the 1968 elections and we were given thousands of proxy forms and were lectured to at PNC offices on how to use them. It was to be assumed that every non-Afro Guyanese was automatically against the PNC and this group was targeted.

We would ask an employee in the office where any of us worked, 'Are you voting for the PNC?', the answer would always be (for fear of dismissal or victimisation), 'Yes'.

We would then say to this non-Afro Guyanese, 'Well, you wouldn't mind signing this form?' Imagine the consternation on this employee's face as he would hedge and try to make an excuse for not wanting to sign it, but in the end complying. This was no secret exercise; it was open, widespread and something like a big circus. The whole thing was a mockery of the principle of honesty, integrity and decency, but we did it and did it well. Therein lay the beginnings of disrespect, dishonesty and moral degeneration among employees in the public sector.

Let us come to the period of the 1970s when our training in the art of keeping the PNC in power took on new dimensions."

We were instructed to make life difficult for the opposition at their meetings. We were to work alongside the Rabbi's group in heckling and breaking up meetings. When I say 'we', remember that many public servants were also leading members of the Public Service Union!

Then the W.P.A. came on the scene with a bang. For the first time many public servants began to see themselves in the mould the PNC had put us, as committers of indecent and unjust acts. This was a time for self-evaluation and reconciliation to better values.

The PNC was in confusion; their stranglehold had been shattered as many of us began to quietly resist unjust directives. And there were many. Some couldn't change or were afraid to refuse unjust directives.

The climax was reached on May 17th, 1978, when the Opposition parties had a meeting at the corner of North Road and Orange Walk (by Bourda Market). Many of us were present, but by this time had become converts so that instead of heckling, we just listened quietly or cheered.

Suddenly, a mini-bus appeared, and stopped, letting out about 14 persons armed with sticks. Leading them was not only a public servant, but a leading member of the Public Service Union (whose name I have appended).

At the same time another vehicle, a Land Rover, appeared from Robb Street with another set of thugs armed with staves and pieces of wood, led by a steel band leader.

The blows flowed on the crowd like water, as people were felled to the ground.

I saw a Catholic priest thrown to the ground; I could not help but go to his rescue.

The meeting was broken up and the public address system strewn all over the place. Llewelyn John was one of the speakers and he should remember. In fact he should think about the incident when the PNC dangles the carrot in front of him at the forthcoming elections.

Those of us like myself were saved from blows by just shouting out 'Hi Comrade' to our fellow public servants turned PNC thugs.

So in case Mr Munroe and his colleagues were 'unaware' of the inglorious history of many employees in the public sector, they should now publicly regret that members of the Public Service and even some officials of the PSU like myself have been made to do the PNC's dirty work, losing our self-respect in the process. Many, if not most of us, have lived to regret it!

It is not too late for employees in the public sector to re-assert their rights to be true public servants as opposed to being PNC stooges.

One of the first acts required of them at this particular time of the expected election rigging by the PNC, is not to be a party to the dishonesty and to speak out wherever it shows itself, in polling places or in other forms, even if threatened with the loss of their job.

They should become true public servants, true to the code of ethics which is now being bandied about.

I ceased a while ago to follow the dictates of the PNC, and I am happier for it.

"I have kept that article not only for its factual contents which are so vital for us to remember but because the writer exhibited enormous courage. I felt that the writing of the article freed his soul and gave him new life. I am sorry that he did not give his name but whoever he is he must never forget that he has done a great service to the people of Guyana. You were the brain behind all of those divulged activities. I did have a chuckle when he mentioned the part about signing a document. Why was this? It reminded me of when you had those ministers sign their letters of resignation! Who taught you that?"

I was still interested in the de-Europeanisation effort for I do not know that if having a good education, skills, honesty, comporting oneself in a tidy manner, being punctual, having something to eat after work, knowing that the civil service was reliable and dependable, being able to eat my butterflap or white-eye or collar and also roti and dhollpouri; having my fried fish and bread at the railway line at Mahaica, going to the horse-races at Durban Park, putting condensed milk on an Edger Boy biscuit, eating fried garlic pork on Christmas morning and many more simple things were all anti-European. If it were and I enjoyed all of the aforementioned since I was fortunate to have spent my youth in British Guiana before the PNC came to power and started on their misadventure, I had not a single regret.

Now mark you, Burnham had said, ...*Adventurism is the hallmark of immaturity and is often indicative of loss of nerve.*[1] This was said in an article published in the Burnhamite edition of the PPP *Thunder* on 16th April, 1955. The publication put out by the original PPP was called *Thunder*. As mentioned previously, Burnham left the united PPP in 1955 and set up his own party retaining the name of PPP. His faction was now referred to as the Burnhamite Faction of the PPP. This name remained until 1957, when it was changed to the People's

---

[1] p.7

National Congress (PNC). Perhaps Burnham did not remember ever saying this when he started on his adventures to make the small man a real man and in bringing about social change; 1955 had long passed and one tends to forget or repeat the same things one is trying to avoid. Without knowing it the spores of a mouldy destiny were being scattered. I was, however, more grateful for being Europeanised. There certainly was a total misunderstanding of what was European and what was decent, courteous and honest. The less truth in this matter seemed to be more acceptable. I would personally have liked to thank the late King George VI and Her Majesty Queen Elizabeth II as they reigned over my period of stay in British Guiana prior to my taking up studies in Canada in 1960. I know that I am eternally grateful, especially for having attended Queen's College; working in the Geological and Agriculture Departments and being afforded the opportunity to travel in the interior of Guyana. Having been given the glorious privilege to travel and having travelled to many countries and having seen many places I can categorically say in all confidence and with pride that Guyana is one of the most beautiful places in the world and it is still unspoiled. But you cannot appreciate it if you do not know it. Many Guyanese have not seen it as I did and Burnham and his colleagues did not know much about it either and thus could not appreciate Guyana. Their knowledge was superficial. If it were not so then their acts were more than criminal.

Meanwhile, President Jagan was reminiscing about his time at Queen's. He was speaking of how difficult it was to adjust since he came from a small country village to the capital, Georgetown. This was in 1933. As he continued to speak I realized that soon the Assembly would be over and the gathering would dissipate not knowing when again there would be another meeting of the QC clan. What the future held for Queen's was unknown but this congregation was becoming more precious by the minute for as time passed an historical event was being recorded.

Down in Avernus, I needed to complete my assignment. I was pleased with the way the deterioration of the pure water supply in Georgetown had been introduced as a topic. Unfolding before me in the restaurant at the Tower Hotel was a social evolution for the increased use of bottled water in Guyanese society which would continue, and for all intents and purposes remain permanently. An economic opportunity was seized because of the failure of the administration to recognise the importance of a pure water supply system for the community and for humanity as a whole. Charles Darwin had developed his Theory of Evolution without being present at the scene millions of years ago. This social evolution was unfolding right before my eyes and the Burnham promise of social change, although he did not envisage this direction, was taking place. The main drawback to more increased usage of bottled water was that the small (real) man could not afford it and therefore the quest to make the small man a real man had failed since all men, whether small or big, rich or poor, need water to keep alive. The failure to maintain the pure water supply displayed the incapacity of the Burnham administration to cope with the bare necessities of life. It was an administration which had nothing to offer the Guyanese people for their betterment.

The precedent of larceny of the vote was well known and an established practice in the society. Since those in the echelons of power could steal the gem of the political gear of the individual then the stealing of other things was secondary. In a speech delivered at Congress Place in Georgetown on July 16th, 1965, and addressing the Institute of Decolonisation under the title 'Change our Society: Revolutionise our Economy', Forbes Burnham said, *You notice that one of the first things the government has been emphasising is self-help – that people must help themselves. The first thing the government did was, not to go around the world begging for alms or grants or loans, but to seek to have people subscribe to their own development. You may or may not agree with the mechanics of that exercise, but certainly you can recognise that behind that exercise was an attempt by a government to emphasise to the people: 'you don't look up to the boss inside, the first thing you do is to try to help yourselves and rely upon your own devices.*[1] This was the advice being given by the Prime Minister of British Guiana and some people, although much later, would heed that advice and give practical applications. I must not forget that he had used his own devices to maintain and retain power.

I refreshed the memory of the tortured figure before me by quoting that extract from his speech. The slight movement of the lips indicated that he recognised the extract. I said to him, "I hope the intent of your advice to have people help themselves was not for them to go out and perform dishonest acts openly but your example of vote stealing was taken by some as the way things should be done. You had developed your own devices for stealing the votes of the people and nothing was done to stop you. You had endorsed public larceny. You inspired the acts of self-help. Some members of the Public Service did not forget your advice and took it upon themselves to practice self-help by way of their own devices.

"This was rampant in the society. To get a birth certificate or a passport in good time was impossible unless you paid a bribe. Such acts pervaded the society in many quarters, but nowhere was it more apparent than at the Post Office. This treasured institution was placed into disrepute and remains so until this day despite efforts by postal officials to eradicate tampering with mail. Eradication of the criminal acts seems impossible. Your ban on the Guyana dollar and the subsequent unavailability of foreign funds forced the workers of the Post Office to help themselves to the property of others. An honest system which had existed from the time of its inception was destroyed within a short time after your ascent to power. Social evolution was once more taking place and a society was in detrimental transition. The opening of mail and subsequent

---

[1] p.124

stealing of contents have been rampant. No amount of complaints has made an impression. Something that the Guyanese people never experienced prior to your ascent to power is now commonplace. Financial assistance sent by family members abroad to those in Guyana have disappeared in the mail and rifled letters, although containing only words, have never reached their destinations. I can only say that the small (real) man has become, to put it in Guyanese terms, a thief man. This is a part of your legacy, a part of the destiny you moulded. It has been a deadly violation of trust. The Post Office and other institutions were gathering mould."

The apparition looked more agonised. I had opened another wound of which he was well aware. He knew that Guyanese society had been set back years. A mould had been created that was difficult if not impossible to change. In point of fact the early forging of a vortex had begun and the Guyanese people would find much difficulty in escaping. Apart from the look of pain, the apparition did not display any evidence of remorse. Perhaps it was pointless since to remedy the damage done it would be necessary to replace the entire workforce at the Post Office, the innocent and the guilty, and this would be an impossible task. The only solution would be a moral rebirth of the individuals involved and this was almost impossible because of the hardships being endured. A lesson and its successful application had been learnt and developed. The die was cast.

The lack of confidence in the Post Office in Guyana had an effect on post offices elsewhere in the world, since no one was ever sure that the mail would get through to the recipients and the use of the Post Office was avoided. The situation created was not dissimilar to the days of stagecoach robberies in the Wild West of the United States nor the practices of the highwaymen in England. Only the modus operandi was different. The only sure personal mail that had a chance of being successful was that written on air letter forms. Those were devoid of contents other than the written word. They were still, however, dangerous instruments since the writing on them could bear questions enquiring about previous mail that was sent. Hundreds of years of civility and trust had been destroyed in a matter of months. Guyanese abroad who were trying to assist those less fortunate at home were hindered in their capacity to do so since the most economic way was fraught with danger. The alternative methods were more expensive and thus hardships were being endured on both sides.

Speaking to the nation on 26th May, 1969, Burnham had said, ...*Taking into account our size and population it is not an idle boast to say that Guyana leads the world in self-help...*[1] This statement, although taken out of context, since he was commenting on the achievement of building the largest primary school through self-help, was certainly appropriate to those who were in operation at the Post Office since they have held on to their lead position and no challenges seem to be in sight.

In the background the Caribbean legend was repeating a chorus line from 'B.G.War' and it occurred to me that there certainly was no care as to what happens in Guyana. I addressed the figure, "I have a viewpoint on money in relation to the countries of the world. Money is similar to blood in the human system – flowing from one part to another. In other words, it is a method of communication and exchange. Money in the economic system of the world does the same thing. Exchange of goods and services from one country to another can be achieved by the use of money as a medium. Therefore, when your decision was made to stop the flow of the Guyana dollar to other countries and to make it an instrument of currency to be used in Guyana only it signalled the ultimate isolation of the people and the country since the communication and exchange lines were cut. Corruption flourished as people struggled to get hard currency. A slow and painful death was invited. Consider what would happen if circulation of blood to the fingers was stopped by placing a tightly drawn cord at the wrist. The fingers would eventually rot and gangrene would set

---

[1] p.147

in resulting in death to the whole body unless there was an amputation of the arm or a portion of it. I imagine that stopping the flow of money would result in difficult circumstances for a country. Now, mark you, there can be an effort to slow down the flow of blood, but to cut it off completely would be courting disaster. The actions of the boys at the Post Office can therefore be seen as an act of preservation since without a means of communication 'death' was inevitable. Your intention of course was to block not only money but the Guyanese people from leaving and if they did leave then they should do so with only their shirts or blouses on. After all they could leave with only twenty Guyana dollars equivalent – hardly enough for a taxi fare. When it came to personal effects those who had accumulated gold jewellery over their lives were told that they could leave with only two or three pieces. You felt that if they had more then it could be sold and they would have some money to start life afresh. And do not forget that despite the system of collecting income tax by workers paying as they earned you had everyone get a tax clearance certificate before embarking onwards. You truly were an evil man. When Guyanese landed on the shores of other Caricom member states they were humiliated and insulted. Some had to sleep on the floors of airports and endured numerous indignities as they fled from the web of a dark and mouldy destiny.

"The natural outcome from your actions was the evolution of the development of the Ways and Means Committee in order for people to survive – the birth of various mechanisms for people to find a way to communicate with the outside world in order to satisfy their desired needs. From the origin of the Ways and Means Committee sprang forth at Timehri Airport the searches of persons including their private parts to ensure they were leaving empty-handed. The Guyanese people were subject to all of those indignities. I often wondered, if your maladministration was so popular as evidenced by the high percentage of votes received at the polls, why would people want to leave or transfer their money elsewhere? It is a question that boggles the mind." I could see that the figure was not very comfortable and this visit was inflicting extra pain on what was already being endured. Still, there was more to come.

Chapter Eight

"Lumumba is dead. Lumumba, however, will live because the things for which he stood are deeply engraved in the hearts and minds of many of us. People like Tshombe, even if they do not meet physical liquidation, will leave behind them names to adorn a special book that must be written concerning the traitors of the twentieth century,[1] so said you on 17th February, 1961, in addressing the Legislative Council. I can rewrite this portion of your speech as follows: 'Rodney is dead. Rodney, however, will live because the things for which he stood and wrote about are deeply engraved in the hearts and minds of many of us. People like Burnham, even if they do not meet physical liquidation, will leave behind them names to adorn a special book that must be written concerning the traitors of the twentieth century.' As you can see the changes are minor but quite appropriate and as accurate as ever can be. When the speeches in your book are read and compared to your deeds and actions you can very well see that traitor is really a mild word. The world and especially the Negro race has lost one of its brightest stars through political rivalry. Guyana, of course, has suffered the most since Rodney was considered one of her most brilliant and courageous sons. Cut down in his prime, Walter Rodney is gone. What crime did he commit to warrant being obliterated by a bomb shaped in the form of a walkie-talkie. Only you know since you had access to the information pertaining to his death. Entrenched with power in Guyana at that time for sixteen years; supported by the Army and the

---

[1] p.234

Police and backed by Party loyalists you were nevertheless afraid of Rodney and his growing support amongst the people. He found courage to stand up to you and that courage could only be stopped by an act of violence which would send him to eternity. He, as you know, was a fellow alumnus but had escaped your neglect of Queen's. When you won the Guyana Scholarship in 1942 Walter Rodney was now entering the world. On 13th June, 1980, a day that will live in remembered infamy, black people and people of the underdeveloped world lost one of its champions through a most cowardly act. Struggling peoples could hardly afford such a loss but that was no concern of yours. The threat was removed. He had to go and the sooner the better."

And now for the first time in this encounter tears came to my eyes as I spoke of Rodney. On 13th June, 1980, Walter Rodney, who assumed leadership of the Working People's Alliance (WPA), accompanied by his brother Donald, went to collect a walkie-talkie from a member of the Guyana Defence Force. After collecting the device and having been given some instructions to follow, and whilst travelling in the motor vehicle, an explosion occurred and Walter was instantly killed. Donald escaped with injuries. It was said that the donor of the device was a double-agent. No inquest was held. An expert was called in from England to investigate the bombing but no information on his findings was made public. Rodney formed part of the trio of the most brilliant scholars to have left Queen's. The other two were Professor Ewart Thomas and my brother Walter, now a consultant physician. Queen's had nurtured three men who were and are of world class in their respective fields of learning. The fragmentation of that trio left me crushed and devastated. The loss of Walter Rodney made me feel as if I had lost a blood brother. I continued on as a tear rolled down my right cheek and brushed passed my lips, "I would not have known of his death from this wretched place since his absence is very marked. It is quite obvious that he is in another section of the Underworld – much more pleasant I am sure since there were no dastardly crimes in his portfolio. I can only say that Rodney's destiny was moulded by you, adding to your repertoire of destructive moulded destinies. And yet, it is Destiny only, garbed in raiment from infancy to death, who engineers the plans of the master draughtsman Fate. It is Fate alone who from the inception of the fertilised egg charters the course of all mankind, and it is Destiny who has been given the sole responsibility and wisdom to determine the outcome of each individual's stay on Earth.

"Walter Rodney, with humble beginnings similar to your own, unlike you, will be remembered with reverence and fanfare. The people of Guyana will remember him in earnest and will speak of his violent demise, whereas it is only through historical facts that you will be remembered. In point of fact you are remembered only for the distress and hardship brought upon the Guyanese people. Rodney's exposure to public life was short but he was more loved than you will ever be and he will be severely missed. Remembrance will be his companion throughout the ages. As is my custom, I have tried to put Rodney's demise in verse and it reads as follows:

Walter! Walter! Friend of so many oppressed peoples,
You left so suddenly and without fair notice.
Scholarly friend, your loss has left an abyss,
Except among those who have little or no scruples.
You took with you a very special kind of knowledge
Of Africa's children and plundered circumstances.
You brought to our lives the voices of hope and courage,
Teaching us to challenge blatant villainous tyranny.
Betrayed were you by Evil's morning coward messenger,
Unaware and ignorant of the radio's hidden danger.
A true hero blasted to oblivion's timeless territory.
We cried, we mourned, the world was discombobulated,
One of its brilliant minds brutally assassinated.
Another punishing blow Guyana was made to suffer
Since the powerful and cunning did not know any better.

Neglected Queen's is very proud to be the Alma Mater
Of its legendary trio – you, Ewart, the other Walter.
'Groundings with My Brothers' remains today behind
Together with 'How Europe Underdeveloped Africa' and
'A History of the Guyanese Working People 1881-1905'
To tutor us and to open up the narrow, shallow mind.
In honour of your contribution to lessen misery
A martyr's monument will stand for all to see.
Courageous friend and guide, immortality is yours
For always you will be much remembered and revered.
Watch over us dear brother and try to understand
Your welcomed return was to a very tormented land.
'Tis very little comfort now but it is consolation
To know the destroyer has departed from this nation.
Perpetual agony in Hades' vile and dismal chamber
Is his to endure and bear till Hell freezes over.
Farewell dear Walter, farewell dear, dear brother.

"I have named that 'To Walter Rodney' and I shall not ask your opinion even if you could speak."

Meanwhile, back in the Upperworld, Dr Cheddi Jagan was speaking of how the University of Guyana was started using the facilities of Queen's College. He spoke of how through innovative means the university was established in one year when others said that it would take three years. He was stressing the need for innovation in resolving the problems of Guyana. However, it was easy to call on innovation for assistance but the fact of the matter was that through gross maladministration coupled with destructive policies the country and all of its institutions had deteriorated to a state where innovative practices would have only a small impact. The PNC had over two decades devastated the country and the boast was that the party was paramount. I did not believe that innovation could put Humpty Dumpty back again after the great fall.

One would not believe that it was peacetime during the Burnham years when examination is made of the events which occurred in Guyana. The country was not at war, but its economic and demoralised states were as if it had been fighting for years. Having gained its independence from Britain in 1966, it slowly found itself in a position where basic food and consumer items were in short supply or non-existent. During the early period of its misrule the regime had set up an organization known as the External Trade Bureau – ETB (Everything To Burnham) – to replace the commission agencies which imported food and consumer items. Soon after its inception shortages were noticeable. One of the first items to be in short supply was salt and that signalled ominous portents. The birth of the ETB heralded the appearance of endless queues (now called guylines) of people waiting to purchase whatever little was available. At one place there would be a line for cooking oil, at another would be a line for soap and toilet paper, at another would be a line for kerosene and cooking gas, and so on. Around that time began the development of the parallel market, and the evil black market also found a haven.

There were lines all over the place! Sometimes people would just join a line not knowing what the line was for. Never was there such a waste of manpower since workers had to leave their jobs to stand in lines. Sometimes when a provider went home for lunch there was no food to eat since the cooking was not finished because of lengthy delays in lines. Yet, the people took it with neither grumbling nor agitation. They were told by Burnham to tighten their belts every so often. Some people retorted that their belts became so tight that their mid-sections were almost to the point of severing. The guyline syndrome was established and well-entrenched. The PNC maladministration had it all wrapped up as the people lived in fear and very few dared to be outspoken or challenge the regime. The people's mouldy destiny was being fabricated with the plasters of suffering, deprivation and demoralization. A once happy people grovelled for their existence. Those who escaped this tragedy, apart from the emigrants, were worshippers of the PNC and those members of the society who hung their lips where the gravy was dropping. It was Burnham who on 22nd December, 1968, in Georgetown at an open-air meeting at Independence Square, said, *I cannot emphasise enough our intention to create a new society completely oriented towards the people as a whole and based on the principle that man is the most precious of all resources. To this end we will accelerate the process of decolonisation already begun. And when I use the word decolonisation I include in that concept the veritable creation of a new man. I include also a complete break with past attitudes of subordination and differentiation.*[1] There was no doubt that a new man was created in a short space of time. A once contented and happy man, although poor, became homo miserabilis under Burnham's guidance. There was no doubt in my mind that the most welcomed visitors were Night and its companion Sleep. The cloak of Night hid the scars of neglect and want, and Sleep, the lesser partner of Death, provided the anaesthetic which gave a temporary respite before its release for the dawning of the next day which would start the cycle of perpetual drudgery. This was the same Burnham who in his 'Report to the Nation' on 12th July, 1965, said, *It is my conviction that Guiana as part of the Caribbean has a contribution to make to the world, a tale to tell -the tale of how a small nation can act independently without making itself a participant in the cold war – a tale of how a small nation can evolve a way of life of its own – a tale of how a small nation can, with the energies of its people and the assistance of real friends, banish poverty, plan its economy and maintain democracy. This contribution we cannot make, this tale we cannot tell, unless we achieve full independence.*[2] The people of Guyana, both at home and in exile, can comment on the various tales and of the upholding of democracy. The roots of poverty instead of being eradicated were nurtured and fertilised

---

[1] p.61
[2] p.58

by his policies and consequently flourished. Before Burnham's ascent to the throne the Guyanese had never encountered such experiences. It was after independence that the aforementioned events took place.

After the rigged election of 1968, with its counterfeit victory, in another speech, entitled 'Guyana Has Prospered', delivered at an open-air meeting at Queen Elizabeth II National Park on 26th May, 1969, Burnham said, *There are those who are afraid of freedom. They prefer the security of a comfortable subservience to the challenges of national independence. They were afraid of self-government, they were afraid of independence, they were afraid of a government run by the People's National Congress. They are afraid of a republic. They see disaster in any change and tremble at the contemplation of the future. But Guyana has sustained the changes from colony to nation, and has survived and prospered. Guyana has prospered with this government. Under this government Guyana will advance as a republic. The fears of the timid will once more be confounded; the hope of the bold and free will be realised.*[1] Only those who emigrated and history need comment. They have been vindicated! On the question of the objectives of the PNC it was in a radio broadcast on 27th March, 1961, that Burnham said, *The object of the People's National Congress will be to develop the resources of Guiana both natural and human for the good and happiness of the Guianese people, to increase the productivity of Guiana, to ensure the fair distribution of the wealth and produce of our country, to give security to all, to establish real equality of opportunity.*[2] All Guyana knows of the fall in production of rice, sugar, and bauxite; of the deterioration of the education system and the breakdown of social and health services of the country during the regime's maladministration. Sugar, which is one of Guyana's main export products, had to

[1] p.151
[2] p.10

be imported from Guatemala to meet Guyanese needs. There was a distribution of wealth – a few became very much richer and the majority became poorer. With respect to paramountcy, in that same broadcast it was said, ...*The People's National Congress belongs to Guiana.*[1] Paramountcy meant that Guiana now belonged to the People's National Congress.

As Dr Jagan spoke of innovation I wondered how he would solve the problems of morality, corruption, physical decay and all other ravages endured by the Guyanese people coupled with the lack of skilled personnel.

I was not finished in the Underworld and immediately returned to the tortured subject. I was greeted with the voice of the king of calypso singing,

> *...But she walk out like a lady,*
> *High heels, glasses, jewellery!*
> *The straw hat she had on wearing before*
> *She take match and she burn it inside the store...*

I decided that I would address matters symbolised by the dragline in the arsenal of metal surrounding his body. During the late sixties Burnham was advised that a lot of money could be made from the bauxite industry. An economic paper was presented urging the nationalisation of the Demerara Bauxite Company Limited (Demba), a subsidiary of the Aluminium Company of Canada Limited (Alcan). Whatever the paper indicated I am quite sure that a footnote was not present saying that the success of the endeavour would depend on the availability of competent and skilled management. Although ownership was important it was management that would be most fundamental. The nationalisation of Demba would bring about a metamorphosis of the bauxite industry since it meant that it would become the only independent producer in the world. The nationalised company would have to sell all of its

---

[1] p.12

products overseas since bauxite was hardly ever used in Guyana. Furthermore, there was a need to shift the emphasis from being a bauxite producer to a producer of refractory raw materials. The sales of metal grade bauxite and alumina were totally dependent on the multinationals since they were the companies which had the facilities for conversion to metal. Refractory grade bauxite was being sold to independents all over the world. It was also the most lucrative of the products being sold. Nationalisation meant that there would need to be a fundamental change and this would require experienced and skilled management personnel. There were not many Guyanese who satisfied those requirements.

The nationalisation took place and many expatriates were retained and new ones hired to assist in the running of the company. This was in keeping with a statement made in Burnham's radio broadcast of 27th March, 1961. It was said then, *The PNC has always held as one of its cardinal principles, Guianisation. That is, that wherever there is a post or an office, it should be filled in the first place by a competent Guianese. If, however, such a person is not immediately available, one from outside can be employed while a Guianese is being trained to take over the post. On that we have no compromise.*[1] The 1971 nationalised company, known as GUYBAU, was performing satisfactorily until it was jolted in 1974 by an edict which stated that all expatriates who wished to continue to work in the bauxite industry could do so provided they were agreeable to accept payment and conditions similar to Guyanese. There was an exodus of personnel from almost all areas of the company and nowhere was it felt more than in the area of mining. Such an edict should only have been given if there was absolute surety that departing personnel could have been replaced by personnel with similar skills or preferably better. It was an edict that was premature by many years. Its consequence was the eventual demise of the industry.

---

[1] p.12

After the rigged election of 1973, and another counterfeit victory, Burnham made sure that the PNC secured more than a two-thirds majority of parliamentary seats. He garnished over seventy percent. He thus had absolute power and felt that nothing could have stopped him. No resistance was offered and the world stood by and let it happen. The country was becoming worse off as the days went by but President Burnham was getting more popular according to the votes counted after the polls had closed.

Having regained my composure, I reminded the figure of his statement on Guianisation and then posed several questions, "Did you really believe that after only three years as a nationalised company that the skills and expertise required to manage this most important industry could have been acquired? How long did it take you before you became silk? Did you believe that because you were giving important jobs to young persons that you could do the same in the mining industry?" The figure gave me a look as if to indicate that he did not realise that others were aware of his appointments. I continued on. "Do you remember when you received a delegation in 1977 of four of the top technical personnel in the Company who were stationed at Linden? Do you recall them telling you that unless there was a change at Linden the industry would be seriously jeopardised? Do you recall the delegation telling you that in a short space of time there would be mining problems?

"And do you recall what action you took? Let me remind you! You sent one of the delegates to head the Rice Marketing Board. You sent another to the Guyana National Engineering Company. The third delegate seeing the writing on the wall did not wait for reposting but emigrated to the United States of America as he had his Green Card. The fourth delegate remained on but was later fired for giving a double increment to a deserved worker. In his case the visit to you was resented and was kept in a favoured breast until that resentment was appeased. Imagine your actions knowing that you did not have enough experienced personnel in the Company and in the country for that matter! And to think that it was one of the most important of industries!

"I need not remind you that when the bauxite industry was nationalised in 1971 that its world-wide market share of the sales of calcined refractory bauxite was over eighty-five per cent. In 1978 when there was a fall in production, despite the commissioning of a new calcining kiln in 1976, that percentage fell to below sixty-six per cent. As the years went by market share continued to fall. Do you know what it is today? Before I tell you the answer let me remind you that those encumbrances, with the aid of the barbed wire, when disturbed inflict severe pain and I know that the answer I will give you is going to be shocking. So brace yourself! The answer is seventeen per cent." No sooner had I uttered those three last words when I saw a small and slow movement of the dragline. It was a reaction that caused the barbed wire to nudge the neck of the apparition. There was a further look of pain on his face. My warnings did not help as the dragline continued to move. It was very upset on hearing the percentage.

I continued on in my conversation, "Chinese bauxite now commands over seventy-five per cent of the market and there is new competition from Brazil. You perhaps did not know this, but when Guyana had that dominant position at the time of nationalisation Chinese bauxite was around but nobody wanted to use it. Apart from being very hard it was not as good as ours chemically. However, when the shortage of our calcined bauxite occurred the refractory manufacturers decided that they were not going to shut down production nor send home workers. They decided to use the poor quality bauxite from China. They were encouraged by its price which was very much lower than ours. There were attempts on our side to transfer the guyline syndrome overseas. You know, the customers could wait for supplies and then stand in lines. This did not work as the customers learnt how to use the Chinese bauxite. Since those early days a lot of research money has gone in to the development of Chinese bauxite and the price is still very much lower than ours. I want to tell you of one of my experiences at the time when the production difficulties had just started. I was at a meeting in New York where the President of one of the largest refractory producers was making an effort to get a commitment from us on the quantity of bauxite his Company could get. During the discussions our lead speaker in all his learnt arrogance asked the gentleman, 'What would you do if I did not sell you any bauxite?' The gentleman calmly said that he would ask for an excuse to use the telephone and call his research people and ask them how his company could get along without Guyana bauxite. That company had purchased about 29,000 tons of bauxite from us the year before and their highest purchase ever was about 49,000 tons. Today, I do not think they buy more than 10,000 tons. With a spokesman like that the industry was in very serious trouble. Its future was grim and also sealed."

The dragline shifted a little more with resultant pain to the phantom. I could see it in his face and it appeared as if he was urging me to stop. However, I continued, "When those boys came to see you to foretell of problems in the industry they were really crying out for help. They were like little children looking to their father for comfort and assistance. You recall that nothing could be done in the country without your consent. Only you could have stemmed the tide. You chose to ignore them, feeling that they were troublemakers, and from that simple rejection the bauxite industry started to crumble and today it is grappling for its very existence. You are aware of the mothballing of the alumina plant in 1983. There is no more production of alumina. Sales of metal grade bauxite do not have a tremendous financial impact. The aforementioned facts are indisputable. However, I want to give you a little credit. Your decision to engage Philipp Brothers of New York was the only sound move you made to your benefit. I say this because if it were not for Philipp Brothers the industry would have crumbled earlier. Philipp Brothers held it together through customer relationships and their advancement of payments. But they could not stop the fall in production and the gross mismanagement that took place. As middlemen Philipp Brothers could not be surpassed. For your information, two years ago expatriate management was brought in to manage the company. The Philipp Brothers relationship was terminated in 1989. The local boys tried to run it but after three years help was needed. Full circle I would say. Another thing that you should not have done was change the name 'Guybau'. You could have retained that name and called Linden 'The Linden Works', and Everton 'The Everton Works'. Guybau was already established and known in the business world. It is like Pepsi-Cola or Coca-Cola changing their names. It would be a disaster! In all fairness, however, I do not think the retention of 'Guybau' would have made things any different. I must also inform you that the sugar industry is also under expatriate management. The history of the sugar industry since nationalisation is similar to that of bauxite. Poor management. Bookers is back managing the sugar industry after you nationalised their interests in 1976. Your local appointments could not do the job and the industry was almost ruined. The irony about the management is that a Guyanese who has worked with Bookers in Guyana after graduating from university and who is also an alumnus of Queen's is the man in charge. He opted to stay with Bookers when the nationalisation took place. Many other Guyanese could have had key positions in the country and assist in its development but your brand of politics drove them away. When I tell you this country had talented people I know what I am saying, and now they are scattered all over the world helping others. Guyana has reared them for other countries. Before I change this subject I want you to know that the nationalisation of the bauxite industry did not result in any ill feelings by purchasers of the products offered for sale. Support was given all around the world but the damage to the industry was all self-inflicted. Having lost so much of the market share it is almost impossible to regain it. It would be a miracle. It is like yesterday's beautiful sunset: It cannot be brought back."

Although I could have gone into the bauxite industry further I decided that I had to move on to other topics as my time here in the Underworld would soon be over. I only wanted the apparition to know that failure of the two main industries belonging to the people of Guyana was due to his actions and in most cases inactions. He was aware at all times of how the industries were failing. It was common knowledge but he continued to keep the square pegs in round holes. It is good to be clever but there really is no substitute for experience in all matters, politics included. Continued clinging to inexperienced party boys in top management was causing failures in the top two industries and others. Those failures resulted in those organizations, instead of making contributions to the national coffers, becoming cancerous as they had to be subsidised, bleeding funds from an already impoverished treasury and resulting in increased pressure on the people. Their losses were huge. The nationalisation had failed not because of the products that were produced but at the hands of incompetence and mismanagement. I can say with the utmost confidence and authority that Guyana's calcined refractory bauxite produced at Linden will always be the best in the world, whether 200,000 tons or 500,000 tons are sold. It is the Rolls Royce of refractory bauxite and it is a shame that it has lost supremacy in the market-place. I can only ask, "Who killed the golden goose?"

Back at the rostrum in the auditorium Dr Jagan was stressing the need to weld the natural resources to the human resources available. He was pleading for the development of our human resources and saw that education was important in achieving that goal. He further stressed that the educational institutions should encourage students in agriculture and agroprocessing and the present day thought that agriculture was drudgery and dirty work be eliminated from the minds of those who thought so.

Chapter Nine

In this dismal Hall of Hades, my eyes glanced at the encumbrance shaped in the form of the electricity works at Kingston in Georgetown. As a youth I do recall an occasional blackout of electricity but nothing could compare with what was happening in independent Guyana. Power cuts were an everyday affair and the damage inflicted on electrical equipment was severe, resulting in losses of spoilt foodstuffs and expensive repair and/or replacement costs. Burnham in the previously mentioned 22nd December, 1968 speech, had said, *The hydro-power project at Tiboku will liberate vast areas of our hinterland for forest exploitation as well as provide employment for our people during the various stages of construction.*[1] This hydropower development was also meant to supply Georgetown with electricity. I addressed the phantom, asking, "What of the hydropower facility you promised? You were advised by my brother Sam on what projects should be attempted but you in your wisdom chose to embark on what I now called the unfinished current effort – 'the grandiose plans for a large scale facility on the Upper Mazaruni River added to the bankruptcy of Guyana which today is still without any hydropower to assist in the development of the country'. You wanted a 3000 Megawatt facility. You will recall as the path was cleared to the hydropower site and no asphalting had taken place fresh growth took over and the pathway was no longer to be seen. The rate of growth of plants and trees in the tropics is astounding. There was no need to embark on such a large

---

[1] p.62

project but then again you never believed in starting small. You truly believed that one could walk from the cradle without intermediate steps. The Tiboku Plan would have given you the power needed and it would not have eaten up the funds that were available. You were always, however, inclined to go for the big things in life, for example, the Austin A70 and the DeSoto. This was before you ended up with the Austin Princess. Some advisers, including my brother Lyttleton, even told you how to generate steam in order to run the turbines instead of depending on oil imports. Their advice went unheeded. This lack of guaranteed electrical power put you at a disadvantage for after you died there were serious efforts to have your body preserved like that of Lenin but with the power cuts the refrigeration system could not keep your body from decaying. The body was sent to Russia for the experts in this type of work to preserve you, but they could do nothing since the carcass had rotted too much. However, they did the next best thing and you came back looking like yourself." Once more the figure winced with resultant pain.

The development of a country can hardly take place without electrical power. Guyana today experiences a lack of adequate power to pursue its development and unless this situation is remedied the country will only progress slowly if at all. Investment and construction require that there be adequate power and priority must be given to this area of development. The situation is akin to an automobile without roadworthy tyres. You may travel a little distance but you will not reach your destination until the tyres are changed. Constant stopping to repair the tyres is not only frustrating but non-productive.

Proceedings in the auditorium continued to move and I could hear Dr Jagan asking alumni to contribute a part of their earnings not only for rehabilitating Queen's but to the national coffers for the development of the country. It was a difficult request since alumni faced financial problems also. What he seemed to have forgotten was that Guyanese abroad were sending home barrels of care packages and were it not for their contribution the situation in Guyana would have been very much worse than it was. Providence had arranged for those emigrants to help the unfortunates at home. Many abroad were working at two jobs so as to manage their own households and lend assistance to loved ones in Guyana. The recipients of their help can never express their gratitude enough. This part of his speech signalled to me that soon he would be finished and the ceremonies would come to a close. I had to get a move on in the Underworld.

Seeing the Lady Thompson Ward encumbrance on the chain around Burnham's neck brought back memories of times I had spent at the Public Hospital, Georgetown. For a small country the PHG, as it was called, was not a bad place. Today, I am told that if you do not want to die stay away from the place. I had made my first visit there when I was about five or six years old and it was in connection with the time I had been kicked behind my ears by a cow. Surgery was performed there on an abscess that had developed and the doctor who saved my life was Dr Grayson. Every time I hear the song 'Tom Dooley' being sung, I say to myself: "Hadn't it been for Grayson I would have been in a cemetery." I spent about a week in the Children's Ward. I visited the PHG on other occasions several times and my remembrances recall that I received adequate and good treatment. The hospital had capable Guyanese and expatriate doctors and surgeons and supporting staff. However, the Burnham years saw the exodus of many doctors and nurses and the institution commenced its descent to becoming a very poor facility, hardly adequate. It was at this hospital that Burnham went for his operation and it was here that he died. Justice was keeping a watchful eye.

I accosted the apparition, "Do you remember what happened at the PHG on August 6th, 1985? Sure you do. It was the day on which your application to this chamber was processed and accepted at the Lady Thompson Ward. You know, as a youngster growing up I had occasion to visit that hospital several times and I always came out alive. Of course in those days it was not run down as it is today. I do not even recall having ever seen a Cuban doctor there. As leader of Guyana it was incumbent upon you to see that our health institutions remained in the best of condition and that there were competent medical personnel available. It used to be like that before you took power. Some great Guyanese doctors practised there but I know that you are aware that they left since they were not happy at the way you were moulding events. The smell was getting worse than usual. I have heard of babies being bitten by rats at the PHG. Without the rats, the infant mortality rate is still very high and you would think that a country with a small population such as ours would treasure every child that is born. I know it is too late now – much too late – but if you had not allowed the hospital to drop in standards I am sure you would not have signed your application for entrance to Avernus at the Lady Thompson Ward. Maybe you would have settled comfortably into The Residence or at the Belfield retreat which I called 'Burnham's Camp David'. By the way, the talk around town was that the government was paying a handsome amount of money in rent to the resident landlord. Imagine that! The place was rented back to the government. I venture to say that only the accountants at the Treasury can verify that story. If it were so then you were nobody's fool – always smart and way ahead!

"Now, I must be honest with you about my feelings on receiving news of the event. When I heard of your acceptance to one of the Halls of Hades, I felt as if a weight which was resting there for a long time was taken off my shoulders. I was in Japan at the time and received the news in Osaka whilst checking in at the Osaka Prince Hotel on August 7th, 1985. The news came by telex and when I heard it I left my travelling companions and went by a window and looked outside. Normally, one should not feel happy at someone's death but with yours I really felt relieved and I was so glad for my fellow Guyanese. Afterwards, when we went out, I believed I spent the most enjoyable night I ever had in Japan. It was a day of

140

deliverance. People will tell you if you had access to them that I never had anything good to say about you after the first rigging. I knew then that if you got away with that then Guyana was in serious trouble. Your death made me remember the movie *The Wizard of Oz* and I pictured the happiness of Dorothy when the wicked witch of the west died. My feelings were not dissimilar and perhaps even more euphoric."

The figure was unmoved. He was aware that his demise was brought about by his actions and in this case inactions. I knew my time was coming to an end but I could not leave without reading to my subject a poem which I was working on. It was not complete but most of what I wanted to say was incorporated. I addressed the painful figure, "Banjoboy, my time down here is coming to a close but I want you to listen to this poem that I am working on. I started on it this morning before attending this function so it really is in draft form but I think it has possibilities. I have not given it a title as yet.

Oh! B.G. dear,
What has become of thee?
Land of my childhood, joyful days,
How changed you have become!
How did you get to this unhealthy state?
Oh land of mythical eldorado fame!
Once you were traded like stamps or merchandise
By actions of Dutch, French and British powers.
Known as the Land Of Many Waters,
You harboured South America's first railway.
Thy rare one cent magenta of 1856 that left in 1873
Remains the most valuable stamp in our history.
Today, only thy rivers and lakes remain intact;
Thy name and electoral system have been changed;
Thy Motherland left thee on thine own
To be governed by wanting, ignorant clowns.
The railway went to dinosaur's realm,
Its iron bars sold off as wealthy scrap.

A means of transporting weighty freight
Destroyed for filthy lucre.
Your new name was hardly known abroad,
Honest work denied as tourism was outlawed.
But tragedy catapulted you to fame
From the portrait left by People's Temple Jones.
Oh what a way to earn thy fame!
Too many of thy learned folk did flee,
Leaving behind the smooth and slippery tongue,
Gone to places which least require them,
Escaping indignities, indiscretions, harassment.
They left in search of freedom and contentment.
To take their places were returning in droves
The once eradicated malarial mosquitoes.
Neglect of property and institutions too
Are legacies of thy 'Flounder Leader'.
Those beautiful wooden buildings left unkempt
For want of small repairs and brightening paint.
Granted an enviable exit permit, Democracy
And banned items took unattainable flight,
Leaving thy people under stress and strain
To bear the burdens of suffering, hardship, pain.
I remember some words of a song I sang
When I was very innocent and young:
'Onward, upward, may we ever go.
Day by day in strength and beauty grow,
Till at length we each of us may show,
What Guyana's sons and daughters can be.'
Today, a different song resounds aloud:
"Backwards, downwards, no progress to show,
Year by year the economy gets more slow,
Till at last we each of us have seen
What rigged paramountcy can come to mean."
Confirmed by all the faces in the crowd,
This land which had such burgeoning youth,
Thrown back decades by a hostile brute!

Never did the powers stand at the front
To do their mischievous and dastardly deeds,
Always delegating to other criminal followers
The task of destroying the people's flowers.
I weep for thee, oh land of my birth!
A place where living was so pleasant, so nice
That I can surely say, 'I lived in paradise!';
Endowed with rich resources of this planet Earth:
Sugar, rice, bauxite, gold, seafood and timbers hard.
Only wise guidance needed to reap the reward.
Deceived by words of flattery at best,
For most of three decades in tormented rest.
Dictatorship, misrule, corruption, falling currency
Are some of the bitter fruits of thy legacy.
Independence removed you from colonial occupancy
But your future prospects did indeed look good
Until the grab for absolute power did ensue,
Robbing you of growth, development, prosperity.
There were not many ways to rebel or shout,
Opposition and newspapers forced to stay lockout.
A brilliant son blasted to eternity.
The dictator entrenched himself very much more.
But no dictator can succeed in his plans alone,
For he needs to have support to keep his throne.
Army, police, civil service, judiciary, People's Militia,
Rabbi's Clan, Cold War fears and
Unions too lent assistance in suppressing you.
So much so the Party of National Catastrophe
Boasted boldly of its ultimate paramountcy.
Alas! Partial relief came in nineteen eighty-five
Through the intervention of Pluto's grim reaper.
Another chance has come thy way once more.
Call October 5 of ninety-two 'Deliverance Day'!
Celebrate always the first Monday in October,
Giving thanks for harvest and democracy's return.
Oh land that promised so much to all!

Your future within a vortex spins,
Climbing towards the whirling top
But unable to reach its freedom rim.
Moral decay, corruption, and financial debt
Keep thee always in a circle pinned.
Thy people have lost the art to discern
The principles of common right from wrong.
No longer do they listen to learned words
But throw their lot behind the racial cords.
Unless better wisdom does prevail
Progress will come slower than a snail.
A mouldy destiny has been left for you,
And relatively little has been told.
New beginnings have now been offered thee
So chart a course based on true democracy
And draughtsman's Fate will steer thy new
Destiny, remembering always to play fair,
Forgetting not to remove the bodies to another
Sphere, for Truth, guardian of the free, sits
Without sweet sleep in Judgment's chair."

I addressed the phantom once more, "I hope I did not bore you with the contents of my verse'. I am not sure what title I must use but I shall store 'Guyana's Plight' or 'Guyana's Blight' at the back of my mind. I would like to tell you of the change in presidency.

"After your entry into Hades, Desmond Hoyte took over as President, and fortified his position in the general election which followed, as the same mechanisms which you left – contrived electoral lists and fraudulent voting – remained in place, and the Hoyte Government was elected with a majority greater than what you had. In other words he was a bigger counterfeit President and therefore started out on the wrong foot. But since that was the system and nothing could be done the Guyanese people had to bear their cross. Now Desmond Hoyte, the Silver Fox (for that is how he was called as his hair was grey), started to change things and reversed some of your master plans. It took some time but he started on de-Burnhamisation. One of the best things he ever did was to free up the currency situation and allow money to flow freely. The communication network was finally reopened. Some people said that he wanted to get Guyana back to how it was before you came to power, but that was an impossible task. I mean to say you know the story of Humpty Dumpty and Guyana's position was similar. There was a small improvement as people were able to speak out and did not feel threatened with fear as was the case when you were there. They felt free. Hoyte started particularly on a programme of state divestment, changing ownership of the nationalised organizations, although he did say at the sixth biennial congress that he would never denationalise. That was only political talk. Is it customary for politicians to say one thing and do another?

"In the meantime, the world was moving on and lots of changes were taking place. One of the main ones was the breaking down of the Berlin wall and the reunification of West and East Germany. That was very much welcomed in the free world. Another big event was the breaking up of the Union of Soviet Socialist Republics (USSR). There are now fifteen separate states. It all happened fast and it also left a lot of confusion. The countries involved in the separation were going to embark on a market economy. It would call for a considerable adjustment and sacrifice but the United States of America indicated that financial and technical assistance would be forthcoming. These two big events brought about an end to the Cold War, which as you know was still in existence during your time upstairs and because of which you were able to get support from the United States of America through the Central Intelligence Agency (CIA) in your quest for power.

"The Cold War being over, the United States decided that the countries of the world should start to do things democratically and that fraud and chicanery should now be stopped, especially in this hemisphere. In the case of Guyana, it was felt that elections should be free and fair in the future. I have always felt that when it comes to Guyana the United States should play a greater role for were it not for their intervention in 1963, prompting the British to change the electoral system, Guyana may not have ended up as witnessed. The United States should welcome any Guyanese who wants to leave Guyana because having given support in installing you they contributed to the misfortunes of the Guyanese. Their recent intervention into seeing that elections would be free and fair is only a partial compensation. However, there is no need to tell you that such news was not music to the powers in the PNC. However, the people of Guyana welcomed the news and were more than happy. For me the news gave me new hope. I even thought of going into politics myself with the formation of a new political party. Banjoboy, I wanted to form the Party of National Unity and my party symbol would be the key, since I envisaged the solutions to the country's problems. I was going to institute some positive, welcomed changes in Guyana with sound and competent management. One of the things I was going to do was to set up a separate department to handle immigrants and returning Guyanese since the country was going to get out of the quagmire it was in and start to grow, and for growth you need people. The maximum unemployment rate that I would have tolerated was five per cent.

"Do you remember how in 1967, one year after independence, you tried to get the British Government to pay the passage of all West Indians who would have liked to come to Guyana? You told Sir Lionel Luckhoo, the High Commissioner, to approach the British Government and that he must also tell West Indians that they should come back to the sun and that Guyana was teeming with jobs. It was quite obvious that Sir Lionel was not sufficiently persuasive. Do you not see now that it was a good thing that the British did not embark on that adventure? What a catastrophe that would have been? Unlike you I was not going to make promises that I could not keep.

"I was going to abolish personal income tax; and I was going to remove those burdensome duties and consumption taxes and replace them with one tax, which would not have exceeded twenty per cent. I would also have introduced a heavy Death Tax. I was going to allow the people to make all the money they wanted whilst alive and when death came I would collect. The ideas were very revolutionary. However, I did not form the party, and it was a good thing that I did not venture into that forum because the results of the elections that were held showed that your legacy was close to being a permanent one. I will explain to you what I mean as I go on.

"The United States of America contributed to the return of democratic, free and fair elections by sending former President, Mr Jimmy Carter, to have discussions with President Hoyte to set up the machinery for the elections which were held in 1992. One of the fundamental achievements was the counting of votes at the polling stations. The Silver Fox was trying to insist that the Guyanese people did not know how to count in many places! Of course you and I know that when those ballot boxes are being transported to the places where those Guyanese who can count abound strange things happen during the journey. I heard that ballots changed places similar to when you change dollar bills for coins. Another great achievement was a new and acceptable electoral list. That electoral list matter reminded me of something I read in a book. It was cited by another author but it was so much to the point. It read, *Even the dead could be called upon: on one occasion a whole cemetery, seven hundred strong, gave their vote, and it was edifying to see that though they had been illiterate in their lifetime, they had all learned to write in their grave.* (Gerald Brenan: *The Spanish Labyrinth*.)[d] I know that you were an avid reader and you must have read that book and tore the page out. The transition to providing for free and fair elections was not easy and there were lots of problems. The preparations were lengthy and the

---

[d] op. cit.

elections did not take place until October 5th, 1992. Observers from all over the world came to witness the election. It was democracy in action. Something that you never tolerated.

"Years before in 1977 I was preparing a letter to send to Mr Patrick Moynihan, the US Senator, after reading in *The New York Times* some comments he made about free elections. I have kept the draft and the contents of the letter were as follows:

Dear Mr Moynihan,

Re: Comment on 'Events in India', page A12,
New York Times, Wednesday March 23, 1977

I would like to correct your views about the states which have been able to change governing parties by free elections. You mentioned Guyana and this is quite true for the general election held in December 1964 when the governing People's Progressive Party (PPP), led by Dr Cheddi Jagan, was replaced by a coalition of the People's National Congress (PNC), headed by Mr Forbes Burnham, and the United Force (UF), led by Mr Peter D'Aguiar. For Guyana that has been the last 'free election'.

Two general elections have been held since. One was in 1968 and was so rigged with overseas voting and padded lists that even cows in a pasture voted. The PNC won a majority, thus eliminating the need for a coalition, which by the way was whittled away in the governing years between 1964 and 1968. The election was 'free' but the counting of the votes was another matter and I am afraid that's where it's all at.

In 1973 the other general election was held and the rigging that took place then was so outrageous that the governing PNC took not only a majority but over two-thirds of the parliamentary seats so that it was free to change the constitution at will. The rigging there was blatant and it had to be as the ruling party was losing heavily as many of its supporters, knowing that the election results would be rigged, were full of apathy and didn't even turn out to vote.

But I would like you to ponder on this. Imagine one of your supporters going to vote for you last November and on meeting the elections officer your supporter was told that he had already voted.

You are correct in saying that the change over in 1964 was very democratic and fair and free. But since that time I really can't agree with you that the elections have been free in Guyana. In fact, I fear for that country and sometimes wonder what the future will hold for a country in which the basic foundations upon which governments are elected are tampered with and the voting process is just a gimmick.

Very informed sources say that what happened in the recent elections in Jamaica was not without the help of Forbes Burnham.

James W. Ramsahoye

"I never sent the letter for fear of victimisation but my comments in the first to last paragraphs signalled how concerned I was about the future of Guyana with you at its head.

"The PPP joined up with a group called the Civic to contest the elections. Other prominent contestants were the Working People's Alliance (WPA) and the United Force (UF). When those elections were held I was in Europe. I had some ideas about how the election results should turn out. Of course, I was thinking of how the country had gone from a nice and beautiful place, to a living purgatory since your ascendancy to power in 1964, and this was the time to show the world that no more will the PNC be given a chance to have much say in the future governing of Guyana. I expected them to get some seats.

Was I ever so wrong? They exhibited a very good showing. It was a case of either poor memory or racial voting. I thought the WPA would have performed better, getting perhaps about twelve to fifteen seats. Banjoboy, they barely made one seat." I thought I noticed a wry smile on the face of the shadow. "As to the UF, they were wiped out. The voting went along racial lines. According to those results the PPP need not have joined up with the Civic Group. The message sent by the election results was loud and clear. You see now why I was glad that I did not form any political party. I would have lost not only my deposit but my shirtjack and pants too! Are you beginning to understand some of the lines in the poem, which is not complete as yet? That is why I could never understand how you could win an election outright with the votes being counted fairly especially after the banning exercises and in such a short time. The vote-rigging that took place could have had a modicum of defence if the country were progressing and making strides, but you knew that as each day passed the country was tumbling fast like Kaieteur Falls to take up the position at the bottom of the economic ladder in the world, and it did finally succeed in holding that position.

"Banjoboy, you were not very bright when it came to developing a country. Sure you were the best public speaker and you had charisma. It ended there. Now both you and Cheddi did not understand that Guyana is a small country despite having an area of 83,000 square miles or about 215,000 square kilometres. You see, it is small because when you came to power there was only one PPP and the population was a little over 800,000. It is only your land space that is big. It is the number of people which tells how big you are in the political world. Guyana has a say in world affairs but not a big one. When I was at Queen's I kept telling some of my classmates and friends that Marx and Lenin were in the right place when it came to B.G. – dead. Their postulations were not applicable to a big country with a small population, especially a country which has bountiful rich resources. What was needed was the common sense to know what to grow and produce and how to manage thereafter! In point of fact the population of Guyana is too small and it will always present a problem when it comes to development. So you see, Guyana did not need to know much about political ideologies such as communism, capitalism, socialism and any other kind of ism. Certainly there was need for capital, but if you have resources money will turn up. To my mind the most important ingredient was freedom of the people to go about their business. Any government in power would have to draft laws and pass legislation to assist the people in making progress. In return, through fair tax laws, the government would get revenues to look after education, health, social programs, infrastructure and matters of national concern. I am telling you that if you leave the people alone and do not encumber them with restrictions and burdensome taxation the country will progress.

"You had travelled so much when you went on those safaris with so many people commandeering for days the single aircraft that was in service. The people had to wait until you returned in order to travel. Commercial airlines were not good enough for you. You remember how your delegation was bigger than those of some of the biggest industrial and economic powers? You visited various countries and thought you could adopt some of the things you saw in those countries; for example, the cooperative system you saw in North Korea, forgetting the culture and unity of the North Koreans. Furthermore, you have seen the way of life in both North and South Korea, and it differs like night from day. Similarly, you knew what life was like in the Communist world, and you knew what life was like in the Western world, and you decided to go the hard route. Have you forgotten the type of aeroplane you used to run the air service of Guyana with? I called them 'Toppleovers'. Maintenance was always a problem. When I think of passenger planes the first names that come to mind are Boeing and McDonnell Douglas. Remember what you said on 26th May, 1969: *We are a developing country but we cannot, we must not, seek to create a replica of any of the developed countries. We have our own problems, but the developed countries have theirs too. There is no perfect country which we can and should hope to copy. We are all seeking a better life and in that search Guyana, guided by realism and goodwill, has as good a chance as any.*[1]

"Whatever happened to realism and goodwill? I think, however, that the most important thing you forgot was that English was our native language. Guyana belonged to the club that spoke the foremost language in the world and you could have been dealing more with countries that had English as their main language. I do not say that you should not have had relations with other countries but my main trading partners would have been English speaking countries, for when I entered into negotiations I would have liked to know that my counterpart used words that I could have found in the Oxford or Webster dictionaries. When I, or my representatives, were finished negotiating, the understanding would be clear. You recall that I spoke of the drinking glasses? That could never have happened to me if I were dealing with an English speaking country.

"Anyway, the PPP/Civic won the election and Cheddi assumed the position of President. He has finally become the headman of an independent Guyana but the Guyana you left behind is in no manner like the Guiana you inherited. I remind you of what your co-editors said in the introduction to your book, *The country's finances were in a mess. According to the British government, the colony was 'insolvent'. In 1962 the Jagan budget produced a $4 million (Guyana) deficit. Two strikes and 'states of emergency' in three years had left the country empty. Unemployment had risen to some 22 per cent and those who were employed by the government were sadly underpaid...*[2] You yourself had said that the country was on

---

[1] p.149
[2] p.xxix

the verge of bankruptcy as evidenced in your 'Report to the Nation': *Some six months ago there were still abroad the results and fears which racial and communal violence had left in its wake. Seven long years of incompetence, ineptitude and corruption had induced an atmosphere of frustration and despair. Our country's economy had become stagnant. Our coffers were practically empty and Guiana stood poised on the brink of bankruptcy. As a nation we seemed to have lost confidence in ourselves. Many had fled from the land of their birth and many were preparing to follow. The workers were disillusioned and could see only unemployment and poverty facing them...*[1] Now let me tell of the inheritance you and your party left for Cheddi after twenty-seven years of peacetime without any day of emergency and not one day of communal violence – a foreign debt of over $2 billion US dollars, and an unemployment rate close to forty per cent: I do not think that bankrupt is an appropriate word. My word is megabankrupt! It is not only the external debt that must be considered but the internal losses due to the failures of the state organizations. I know you do not have your calculator here but that sum of money in Guyana dollars is astronomical. At the time you came to power in 1964 a US dollar was equivalent to $1.70 G. When you left to come down here, one US dollar was equivalent to about $4.20 G if you could get it legally! As I speak the equivalent to a US dollar is about $137 and you can get US dollars legally now if you can afford to buy them. I know that you know a billion has nine zeros behind it and therefore you now can see why I say a debt of $274,000,000,000 G is called astronomical. The public debt you inherited was equivalent to about $80 million US or Guyana equivalent of $136,000,000. In other words the PNC left a millstone around Cheddi's neck, as the prices for our export products are the same as the time you left, or even lower in some cases! Recall how you criticised Cheddi for not

---

[1] p.48

spending and of what you said at the time on July 12th, 1965: *But the ill-judged economising to which we have referred was only one facet of the picture of disarray with which we were faced on taking office. There was another facet – inefficiency and mis-spending as the concomitants of an elaborate system of corruption and nepotism.*[1] He never liked spending and you went overboard. Prior to your ascent to power it was known that you did not pay your debts and there were many who left the Upperworld without being repaid. I had a friend who is down here but in another sector who told me that when you were in power you shouted at him when he told you that the budget did not cater for certain expenses that you wanted to incur. You would tell him, *Budget! What Budget? You s...t better find the damn money!* He also told me of how members of the Overseas Missions were not paid for months. Those unfortunate people certainly endured tremendous hardships. Joining the queue for payment were the landlords and others who had performed other services. On the observation of inefficiency and misspending it is a straight case of a very big pot calling a small kettle black.

"The per capita foreign debt of Guyanese is the largest in the world, so much so that it surpasses that of all the countries in South America. You took the Guyanese people down to great depths. By creating that debt, the PNC actually achieved the Guyana motto of 'One people, one nation, one destiny'. All are in the ship that is struggling to keep afloat; all are economic slaves. According to Sparrow you have been the architect of economic slavery and he did not have you in mind when he sang 'Good Citizen'. Regarding the flight of people there are no concrete figures but I understand that almost 500,000 people left during the PNC regime and you were in charge for over twenty years. I remind you of what you said in that same report to the nation in 1965 and which I have quoted earlier. The one that indicated that you were going to tell tales as

---

[1] p.50

demonstrated by what a small nation can do.[c]   Under you, Guyana achieved independence, but those dollar numbers and the unemployment rate which I have mentioned as part of your legacy to Cheddi are not tales that you would like to tell. They do not even qualify for inclusion in any book by the storyteller J.O. Cutteridge.   Those details are very accurate.   As for democracy you know how that went since you were the draughtsman. I never understood the rigging exercises because in spite of all that power you allowed my people to suffer as the days went by. That I could never understand unless, as I have often said, you did not care one iota for the Guyanese people, but just you and yours. But any man who would have bread taken away and destroyed from people who are trying to have a meal cannot really care. You just did not have an interest." Immediately after I said those words I saw the apparition writhe in excruciating pain as all the encumbrances moved as if they were applauding. I imagine it was the type of pain when your finger is hit unexpectedly with a hammer, or when one of your shins is hit with a cricket ball from a hard drive when fielding close, or when somebody suddenly strikes you so hard that you end up with broken bones.

---

[c] op. cit.

Chapter Ten

Real applause greeted my ears and I knew it sounded the end of Dr Jagan's speech. In the programme provided, the speech was to be followed by a musical interlude supplied by the Queen's College Choir. I had no doubt that the choir would give a good performance since scrutiny of the students on the stage showed that there were more girls than boys. However, they were no match for the Caribbean legend who continued in the background in Hades but who himself was getting competition from the saxophone player.

A woman walk in a store on Main Street,
Slippers on she feet, dutty petticoat, long time straw hat
And she smelling worse than that.
But she walk out like a lady,
High heels, glasses, jewellery!
The straw hat she had on wearing before
She take match and she burn it inside the store.

I don't care if the whole ah BG burn down.
I ain't care if all ah Bookers burn down.
But they'll be putting me out me way
If they tackle Tiger Bay
And burn down me hotel
Whe' all meh wahbeen does stay.

It was sounding so sweet and lovely that only heavy restraint stopped me from jumping up. That would have been too much for Burnham. I wondered if this music pervaded other areas of Hades where it might have been possible for other shadows, not shackled like Burnham, to react in suitable fashion. It would have been a treat to see those disembodied phantoms flouncing. Out of the blue I heard, "Traveller! Get on with it. Your time draws close." The choir sang on.

I thought it would be a good idea to give the bodiless ghost some more news update as to what was happening in the world. To let him know of some other changes that had taken place. I also wanted to tell him of some local events.

I addressed the apparition, "Banjoboy, I have told you about the USSR and East Germany. Soon after the Soviet dissolution civil war broke out in Yugoslavia and the country you knew as Yugoslavia no longer exists. The place is split up into five States and something called 'ethnic cleansing' is taking place as if through killing each other the colour of blood and the origins of man can be changed. People who lived closely with each other under Tito are fighting each other forgetting that the time upstairs is short and enjoyment of life should be the first priority. When the news of what is happening there is shown on television I feel so sad and can only think that mankind really is the worst in the animal kingdom. The brains of some people do not function at all. The UN, NATO, USA and Russia are all involved in trying to bring about peace but without success.

"On the good side, Israel and the Palestinians have been at peace. It has not been that long. Negotiations are still going on and quite a few issues remain to be settled but in the long run it is hoped that a lasting peace will evolve. But your friend (and also a President for life), Saddam Hussein, is under pressure, with the result that the Iraqi people are suffering as United Nations' sanctions are in force.

"Perhaps the best news for you is that Apartheid has been put down in South Africa. Nelson Mandela is the headman there after elections. He has a hard job ahead but all concerned are working eagerly to make it a success. South Africa has been in the wilderness for a long time but what happens there in the future will have a significant effect in the area. Already we have had a visit of their cricket team to the West Indies and it was thrilling since we almost lost the one test match that was played.

"The situation was like this: at the close of the fourth day's play South Africa ended up with 122 for 2 wickets chasing 201 for victory. I was of the opinion that all West Indian supporters went home believing that the West Indies would lose and the ground record of Kensington Oval in Barbados where West Indies have not lost a game since 1935 would be broken. In South Africa the victory celebrations must have started soon after close of play, maybe before. The occasion was as tense as an Alfred Hitchcock movie, but with only seventy-nine runs to make you had an idea of how the ending would be. It was as thrilling as the time when you had Clive (Clive Lloyd) brought to Bourda by helicopter after coming off the plane at Timehri and when he batted he scored a century. Well, Banjoboy, play started promptly at 10.05 a.m. on the fifth day. This is what unfolded. At 10.16 the third wicket fell. Crowd started to agitate. 10.37 the fourth wicket falls. Crowd a little more agitated. 10.48 sees the falling of the fifth wicket. Crowd a little short of being wild. 11.06 and the sixth wicket tumbles. Crowd behaviour definitely more than wild. 11.18 and another wicket falls. The score is 142 for 7. Crowd senses that victory is in the air. 11.32 heralds the falling of the eighth wicket. The crowd gone mad. 11.40 and the ninth wicket bows out. Cannot stop the crowd now. A minor miracle is about to happen. 11.42 and it's all over. Crowd is now known as maddening crowd. Final score: 148. Ambrose 6 for 34, and Walsh 4 for 31. Ambrose is from Antigua and you know that Walsh is from Jamaica. Tell me if you have ever experienced thrills like that in 108 minutes, the same length of time as a thriller movie!?

"Can you believe I missed seeing all of that having gone to the first four days of play. Yes man, I did not expect the boys to pull it off and so I stayed home and was listening to the radio. I missed it all. The times given in the recall are true. The crowd behaviour is my imagination because there was not a big crowd at the ground since most people felt the way I did. I knew you would be interested in hearing about South Africa since your interest goes back publicly when you debated in favour of a boycott of trade on November 18th, 1960.

"Do you remember what you did in 1981 when England was touring the West Indies? Let me refresh your memory. You did not allow the second test match to be played at Bourda because an English player, Robin Jackman, had gone to South Africa as a coach. You thought that there was a breach of the Gleneagles Agreement. Legal luminary that you were, you thought that your interpretation was correct, but it was wrong since later adjudication showed that the Gleneagles Agreement did not apply to individuals. Banjoboy, you wanted to show how much power you had hoping that the tour would have been called off. You were so wrong. However, once again you managed to deprive the Guyanese people from seeing that test match. Oh what hardships my people had to suffer under your stewardship!

"Do you remember Ferdinand Marcos of the Philippines? Like you, he was a President for twenty years. About seven months after you got here, he was toppled and replaced by Mrs Corazon Aquino, the widow of the Opposition Leader who was assassinated by Marcos' troops in 1983. His demise was only three years after Rodney. You know what she said on being installed: 'The long agony was over,' and later on she said, 'A new life starts for our country – a life filled with hope, and I believe, a life that will be blessed with peace and progress.'[f] She is not in power now but the Philippines are progressing. Her words reminded me of how I felt some time before in a faraway place. Marcos is down here in this sector.

"A little before that happened self-styled, President-for-life 'Baby Doc' fled Haiti. His name is Jean-Claude Duvalier, as you recall, and news had it that he was more hated than 'Papa Doc'. 'Baby Doc' left Haiti with close to 200 million US dollars. To me those Presidents-for-life accumulate a lot of money. Can you enlighten me?

"Let me now give you some local news now that we have a new President. The first thing I must tell you is that Hammie (Hamilton Green) was expelled from the party. Hoyte and some of the other fellows did not want to have any more association with him. Well, you know Hammie better than all of us who are still living. He just left the party and formed his own, calling it the Good and Green Georgetown Party (GGG). The party will be taking part in municipal elections and he himself will be running for Mayor of Georgetown. I did not see him in the auditorium nor on any other occasion during these celebrations. Like you, he is an alumnus.

"The PNC held their tenth biennial congress and the theme was 'For Party and Country, A New Vision: A New Hope.' I really do not know much about PNC Party activities so I cannot tell you what happened. But from the theme's title they are intent upon some fundamental changes. I had heard that they were going to put up a revised party constitution which if I remember was suggested by you in former congresses.

"Do you remember what happened to the Post Office during your time? The officials are still continuing to explore anti-tampering measures. That is really a sad case and I do not think that you will ever be forgiven for allowing that organization to tamper with the mail. That should not have

---

[f] *Chronicle of the 20th Century*, published by Jacques Legrand, p.1264.

been allowed to happen to one of the finest services that a government can provide for their citizens.

"The new government has finally decided to set up a Commission of Enquiry to investigate the death of Walter Rodney. This is long overdue but you would not have done anything (for obvious reasons) and Hoyte could not do anything either. I am glad that efforts are being made to resolve this matter. That really was a loss and he was so young. I was terribly hurt when I heard the news. I pondered all day on the fragility of life and how it could be ended so suddenly without divine intervention. One moment you are here and the next you are gone forever. It was like blowing out a candle." A piercing sound seemed to have emanated from the walkie-talkie and the ghost fidgeted.

I continued on with the bulletin, "Her Majesty Queen Elizabeth II came to visit Guyana in February last. You may recall that she visited in 1966 when you were Prime Minister and not a god as yet? She stayed for four days. I understand that Georgetown had a sprucing up but nothing could have been done about the roads which are full of potholes. The difficulty was resolved by steering clear of areas with those cratered strips. In her mind she must have been amazed at the decrepit state of Georgetown when compared to her visit in 1966.

"Gold is turning up now in quantum. It seems as if eldorado is really here. There are some big companies operating in the interior. I read somewhere that a company called Omai pulled out about 207,000 ounces in 1993 and were looking for about 260,000 ounces this year. You really left too early for I know you always had a very special interest in our gold production. My only hope in all of this is that the gold mining operations do not bring about contamination of our clean and beautiful rivers which if it happens will be felt for generations after. Apart from that it would also have a tremendously negative impact on trade of fish and shrimp. Cyanide and mercury are used a lot in these operations and should they be allowed to contaminate the water then death is inevitable. The first to feel its effects are the fish and animals that drink the water. Of course you know all about cyanide poisoning from the Jim Jones affair. Unluckily for the recipients it will not be cyanide masked in kool aid. River contamination will be disastrous because the animals will not know about the contamination and in some instances people will not know in good time. The same can be said for mercury. Gold mining is rewarding and lucrative but it really is fraught with danger and underdeveloped countries do not have the muscle and finance to monitor the operations.

"The Guyana Constitution that you left still stands as it is. Nothing has been done to change or reform it. You know that when it comes to the Presidency in Guyana there are articles pertaining to the President which transforms the incumbent from being an ordinary man to a man who can do no wrong in or out of office. It deifies you. You were really a powerful man in Guyana and you set it up so that you became untouchable like the FBI's Elliot Ness and some other people. You probably had in mind that if by some miracle you were defeated and lost the Presidency then you would not be called upon to answer for those criminal acts associated with the past elections and for other offences. I do not know what Cheddi is going to do about your constitution. I know it is not a valid constitution, since it came about through fraud. A lawyer of your calibre should know that anything obtained by fraud is not valid. That is a big problem for the Guyanese people!

"The border issues that you left are still unsettled. You know that issue was kept alive because of your ambivalence and willingness to flirt with Russia and Cuba. You still did not understand where the power stood. I just hope that we do not lose half the country when all is said and done. You really left that country in a fix – heavy debts and unresolved border issues.

"Cheddi has been asking the Police to do better. The Police do not have such a good reputation. They lost the confidence of the Guyanese people after you came to power. If there were really a strong Police force, some of the things that brought misery to the Guyanese people would not have happened. We needed a Police force like the RCMP in Canada. Those boys would not think twice to bring in a President or government minister if he were found wanting. They always get their man. Our present economic situation is very conducive for the criminal elements in our society. You can recall that crime was very much under control before you took power. Now it's almost like a business enterprise.

"This new government elected under the first free and fair election since 1964 is trying to make more land available for housing. They expect to give out about 1000 acres in the Mocha area next year. Do you remember that piece of land east of Mandela Avenue and behind the Botanical Gardens? Well, the government has set aside that land as a diplomatic enclave. Already the Embassy of the People's Republic of China has given instructions to build. I understand that Viola leased about twenty-five acres at the back of the Botanical Gardens. Hoyte gave her a twenty-five year lease but the new government is not too happy with the arrangements. The land is to be used for farming but you would have thought that with so much land in the country that farming should have been taking place elsewhere and not in that area.

"The United States Agency for International Development (USAID) is back in Guyana, having been closed since 1985. I understand the Peace Corps is to return in 1995, having been away for about twenty-eight years.

"In the line of sports I really do not have much to say. I only follow cricket and I must relate to you that I saw another thrilling game of cricket at the Queen's Park Oval in Trinidad. This time I was there to see it. It was earlier this year and West Indies were playing England. Again it was the fourth day and I was there to see another thriller. West Indies made 252 in the first innings and England replied with 328. In their second innings West Indies made 269 leaving England 194 runs for victory. It was about ninety minutes before close of play when West Indies were out. The England captain was facing the first ball from the pavilion end at 3.40 p.m. when their second innings began. Before 3.41 he was halfway to the pavilion having been adjudged LBW with the first ball. The crowd was really wild! 0 for 1. The over had not finished when the second wicket fell with the incoming batsman, whose father is a Guyanese, headed back to the pavilion after being run out. 1 run, 2 wickets. The crowd in an uproar! Second over from the pavilion end and the incoming batsman returns from whence he came with a cipher behind his name. 5 for 3 wickets. They had to send for riot police! A brief respite for England ensued but with the score on 21 the number 5 batsman heads for a change of clothes having scored 6 runs. The bowler from the pavilion end did the damage. 21 for 4 wickets. The crowd was now crazy! 5 runs later the pavilion end striker hits again and the stumps of the number 2 batsman is left sprawling. He had scored 18. 26 for 5 wickets. All members of the crowd are close to being hoarse! One run more and the bowler at the other end sent back the number 7 batsman for duck after he was caught at first slip. 27 for 6 wickets. The crowd was now starting to erupt! Another short respite and then the pavilion striker returns to send back the number 8 batsman after a fine catch at second slip. He scored 4 runs. 37 for 7 wickets. The crowd still in the eruption stage! It is the last over of the day and four balls have been bowled. The number 6 batsman who was there for 47 minutes and was watching the spectacle felt he was safe. I heard a clunk after the fifth ball had been bowled. Number 6 headed for the pavilion having scored 3 runs. 40 for 8 wickets. The crowd was fully erupted and no one was sitting! Play is ended for the day. The lowest score England ever made was 45 in 1887 against Australia. The lowest ever against West Indies was 71 in 1976 at Manchester. Both records were under threat. The name of the pavilion striker was Curtly Ambrose and his supporting partner was Courtney Walsh. I call them the Dynamic Duo.

"On the fifth day the action continued. It took eighteen minutes to end the game. Ambrose did not take any more wickets but Walsh took the ninth wicket with the score on 45 and he finished off the number 10 batsman with the score on 46. The bowling figures were Ambrose 6 for 24, and Walsh 3 for 16. The Dynamic Duo had done it again. It was a game to remember!

"England got back revenge in the next test at the Kensington Oval in Barbados. They had lost the first three tests but they won the fourth test in fine style. They not only won the test, they broke the ground record which had stood for fifty-nine years. I was of the view that the loss was due to bad captaincy. Barbados was experiencing one of its worse periods of drought and it was very hot. England before the start of the test had just been beaten by an island combination team. Morale must have been low. The West Indies captain won the toss and instead of batting, thus giving the English side some heavy sunning, he chose to field. I am sure that England's captain was praying that he would win the toss so that apart from batting first the team would have a rest. His prayers were answered. West Indies had them on the ropes but failed to capitalise. They eventually lost the test. It was sweet revenge but it was what was to be.

"The breaking of the ground record forced me to put the event in verse, and as soon as I returned home I wrote this composition. I call it 'The Record'.

In 1935 West Indies lost for the first time at Kensington.
Ever since challengers have tried but not a game was ever won.
The record, like a centurion, stood for fifty-nine years;
But on April 8 of '94 those watchful eyes were full of tears.
The oracle foretold that West Indies would have won the toss,
But it could not see that there would be a tremendous loss.
The battlefield at Kensington was parched and longed for rain,
But the Island was void of showers and under heavy strain.

Visitors had come before to look at cricket quite a lot,
Now all complained, 'We've never found it so oppressively hot!'
Before the action started the opposing side had felt the heat,
Having just arrived after suffering another painful defeat.
On the pitch the visiting captain prayed for the toss to win,
Or else his sun-tanned team would face another defeat again.
To his despair the toss was spun and he lost once more,
Oh dear! Oh dear! An internal lament hit at his very core.
Why had the Fates been so unkind and cruel as before?
But the oracle knows who is to bat, and who is to field,
And when to victory the opposing team must also yield.
Despair turned to hope when the winner of the toss did say,
'You bat, and I will bowl you out this most eventful day!'
The centurion tried to raise his aged statued hand,
For now he knew the treasured record could no longer stand.
England went on to win convincingly a splendid test.
Confidence restored; and shaken; centurion laid to rest.
Amidst the pain of loss, and the joy of hard fought victory,
The vice-captain of England played to a place in history,
The first Englishman to score in each innings a century,
Since 1930 when England and West Indies met in rivalry.
The victory was a repeat of the outcome of 1935 in January,
The silent record could not hold on for a coveted century.

"The next test that was held in Antigua was a draw, but a twenty-four year old Trinidadian by the name of Brian Lara broke the record of 365 set by Gary Sobers in 1958. He made 375. Later on in the year in England he broke the record of Hanif Mohammad who was the holder of the highest individual score in first class cricket. He scored 501, beating Hanif's score of 499 which was set in 1959. I saw this young man score 167 at Bourda this year and I can tell you that it was one of the most sparkling innings ever seen there. The young man is definitely a batting genius. Just as you had the gift of speech so it is that he has the gift of batting.

"Banjoboy, that is all the news I have to give! I thought it would break the monotony and provide some excitement for you." The shadow was unmoved. It appeared that exciting cricket games did not provide any relief. I was the only excited one. "Unlike Guyana, the cricket teams from South Africa and England have recovered from their routs, but your wreckage of Guyana, coupled with my recent observations, suggest that there may be a hint of permanency."

Chapter Eleven

I wanted to point out to the ghost how devastating the devaluation of the Guyana dollar was on the Guyanese people. I had mentioned before that the people were all struggling in the same boat but I wanted him to know it was even worse.

I spoke to the phantom, "Have you ever heard of being free but you are in prison? Well, the Guyanese people are free but they are imprisoned. They are Guyana bound because of that exchange rate. When I was at Queen's and the August holidays came some of the students travelled abroad for vacation. I have not forgotten going once to Surinam with fellow students as a member of the QC Tour Club for about two weeks. At other times some students even went as far as New York on their own! The Guyana dollar had some value then and of course it was tied to the pound. The situation has changed so much that families cannot take a vacation abroad nor even in Guyana because their earnings have been drastically reduced. Most of the people who travel are those who are doing so on business whether it is a public servant, trader or someone working in the private sector. Any others are those who are travelling on a one-way ticket as emigrants. Let me tell you how this confinement of the family has come about. Take a family of four – husband and wife and two children of school age. Let me use as an example that this family would like to go to New York and see their relatives whom they have not seen for a long time. A good estimate of an adult return economy fare is about $600 US or $82,200 Guyana dollars. For the family of four the fare may be about $2000 US or $274,000 G dollars. The

money I have mentioned is for airfare only. If I changed the
venue to Barbados the cost would be about $800 US or
$109,600 G. Can you see that without the committal of a crime
people are shackled? Only the very rich can think of leisure
travelling, and there is no point for only one member of the
family to travel. What a destiny you have moulded for the
Guyanese people! The same financial constraints do not apply
to our Caribbean neighbours and the workers there put in a
day's work just like the people here. Some of our Caricom
neighbours got their independence a few years before us, but
they have not experienced the devastation that we have seen in
this country. The money received by pensioners who have
worked for over twenty years is sometimes less than $7 US per
month. Look at our resources! And our people were once the
cream of the educated in the Caribbean! What was this destiny
you were moulding? Let me remind you of what you said at
the Parade Ground on 18th November, 1962, *As I said six
weeks ago, independence is not only an emotionally satisfying
status, it is also the vehicle by means of which the people
through their elected representatives can fashion their own
destiny, can change the economic system which under a colony
is orientated outwards to serve the interests of those outside.*

*Independence is the means whereby we can change that
emphasis, revamp our economy and make full use of the
energies of our people in setting up a system where there are no
rich men in their castles, no Lazaruses at their gates whose
sores the dogs of poverty lick.*[1] The energies of my people have
been sapped, and poverty has not only visited them, but like an
emigrant seeking a Green Card, has taken up permanent
residence here." I thought I saw the stool move and that would
have been disastrous for the shade.

I could not hear the choir anymore and that gave the
Sparrow a clear opening to my ears, I heard:

---

[1] p.78

They send for soldiers quite up in England
With big confusion.
They bring down warships with cannon like peas
To shoot Guyanese
But BURNHAM say, "Alright now,
I am the only man could stop this row."
He give we the signal and that's the case.
Now we have peace and quiet in the place.

But I ain't care if the whole ah BG burn down.
I ain't care if all ah Bookers burn down.
They'll be putting me out me way
If they tackle Tiger Bay
And burn down me hotel
Whe' all meh wahbeen does stay.

The head prefect, David McGowan, started to deliver the vote of thanks. Soon after, the hymn would be sung and I would have to leave.

I said to the disembodied figure, "Some people said that you were a man of vision. I can only agree with that in one respect: when you awarded yourself the O.E. I said that you really knew yourself. Looking at those national awards with the various letters of the alphabet being used I wondered why after the Order of Roraima, which as you know is the second highest order, the highest order should not have been O.G. – the Order of Guyana. I thought it was the natural thing to do. But Fate moves in mysterious ways and gave instructions that O.G. should not be used in your case. After the damage you had done to Guyana through the electoral system and having made yourself a dictator, O.G. would not have been appropriate. If Guyana, the country, could have spoken she would have said that you did her a great injustice by bringing her down to the foot of the economic ladder and sowing the seeds of moral degeneration. She would have said 'O.G. was out of the question but O. E. was the perfect award.' Guyana had no hesitation in awarding the Order of Evil to its first dictator. It is hoped that it would be the first and last Order of Evil to be awarded. Awards must always be based on outstanding achievements of merit. The delivery of your speeches in the Upperworld was excellent but the betrayal of their contents gave them the hollow sound of sweet nothings. Your talent for fraud and acts of cowardice surely cannot be awarded with excellence. Be consoled, you are not alone when it comes to men of evil. I am sure there are quite a few down here based on the criteria used for placement." The eyes of the apparition were aflame and he moved a little only to find himself in agony. Down here I could tell him anything provided it was truthful and honest. If it were not so then I was weaving the strands of a similar fate.

I heard the clapping of hands and knew that the hymn was next. My time was definitely running out. Soon I would be out of this murky realm providing I did not linger. I would miss the sounds of the Sparrow but that was not a problem since I had most of his calypsos in my collection of music.

I spoke to the phantom knowing that it would perhaps be my last opportunity to do so, "Banjoboy, my time has come and I must go back to the land of the living. I was glad to have this visit with you and to be able to express my feelings about you and Guyana. In a way I was glad that you could not speak for I feared that if you did you may have dissuaded me from saying all the things I said. You were always so persuasive. Your smooth talk may have gotten the better of me. You are here in a dismal place but it has been of your own making. You still have many followers above and my regret is that they have not fully assessed what you have done to Guyana. They have not examined their hearts and seriously looked at the devastation. We all cherish our attainment of independence, but thereafter our woes started. When you were pleading for independence before the United Nations in New York this is what you said on 3rd March, 1963, *Independence, we feel, is the inalienable right of the people of Guiana. It would mean the final recognition of their human dignity, an end of the long period of foreign rule and domination and an opportunity for them to replace the old, oppressive and dehumanising colonial system by one where there would be real freedom for all and political democracy combined with social democracy. This is the people's just entitlement.*[1] When I recall a statement like that to you and knowing what you have done to Guyana you cannot be surprised that people were leaving by the thousands to find refuge elsewhere. The way you ruled was foreign to the Guyanese people. It was a dreadful replacement. The words 'domination', 'oppressive', and 'dehumanising' are buried with you. They were your stock in trade. As for democracy, there was no room to accommodate any of the kinds you mentioned.

"Some will say that you made us feel proud as Guyanese but we were always Guyanese. I was always proud to be Guyanese even when we were a colony. That could not change. I never felt comfortable being otherwise. Tell me if any other nationality could enjoy a pepperpot or a metemgee with lots of duff (steamed flour product) or a cookup rice with obstacles (meat, pork, chicken, split peas etc.) or a black pudding with plenty of Married-Man pork (a variety of basil) or a souse laced with cucumber and onions. Those are Guyanese dishes and you banned some of the key ingredients. They represent Guyanese culture and were around before you ever saw God's light! There are many other things that the Guyanese do that make them distinctively Guyanese, so do not think that you were doing anything out of the ordinary. We were proud of what we were until you changed us to confirm with our pauperised status and to make sure we were a changed society. In fact, when I compare what you have done to my people, I would say that you acted in a very non-Guyanese manner. It was as if you came from another planet. Guyanese are kind, gentle, caring and friendly people and basically very peaceful. You cannot boast of those qualities. Today the Guyanese experience a

---

[1] p.90

172

different type of slavery. One that is much more difficult to get rid of. It is a bondage which will keep them enslaved for a long time.

"You dragged us down instead of making us prosperous and happy. I am very annoyed with you because you have engineered the splitting of families and the family is the foundation of civilized societies. When I think of my own family and how we are all scattered over this globe I cannot find any charitable words on your behalf. Although it has not taken place in similar fashion and for the same reasons it reminds me of the splitting up of Jewish families during Hitler's reign of terror. Of all the countries that have become independent from the British Crown, Guyana is the only one to have endured such mass migration of its citizens. There are as many out as they are in and they are scattered like airborne seeds which take root wherever they have landed. The Guyanese would have strutted like peacocks if democracy and economic wisdom had prevailed and I would not be visiting you down here. Our population would have surpassed the million mark and we would have been on our way to being a proud nation envied by many others. It was you who said this in 1969 on August 24th, ...*Our material resources are vast, at least in potential. We have forests, rich agricultural lands for crops and cattle, large rivers that can yield a fortune in fish and drive the turbines of hydro-electric plants. Precious stones and valuable metals, which we and the world need, are in the bowels of our earth...*[1] Having recognised that potential and being the ruler of it all how do you explain the circumstances of Guyana? You wanted so much to be the ruler and by your policies and actions you were fast becoming the ruler of a graveyard. I have always maintained that there are no underdeveloped countries, only underdeveloped minds. Guyana's status confirms that, having been endowed with all of those resources – human and natural. I have been reading a

---

[1] p.153

book on Buddhism and I would like to read to you what is said about being a ruler. I quote, '*The duty of a ruler is to protect his people. He is the parent of his people and he protects them by his laws. He must raise his people like parents raise their children, giving a dry cloth to replace a wet one without waiting for the child to cry. In like manner, the ruler must remove suffering and bestow happiness without waiting for people to complain. Indeed, his ruling is not perfect until his people abide in peace. They are his country's treasure.*

'*Therefore, a wise ruler is always thinking of his people and does not forget them even for a moment. He thinks of their hardships and plans for their prosperity. To rule wisely he must be advised about everything – about water, about drought, about storm and rain; he must know about crops, the chances for a good harvest, people's comforts and their sorrows. To be in a position to rightly award, punish or praise, he must be thoroughly informed as to the guilt of bad men and the merits of good men.*

'*A wise ruler gives to his people when they are in need, and collects from them when they are prosperous. He should exercise his correct judgement when collecting taxes and make the levy as light as possible, thus keeping his people consonant.*

'*A wise ruler will protect his people by his power and dignity. One who thus rules one's people is worthy to be called a King.* [g] In your almost twenty-one years of ruling you never came anywhere close to that mould and it is quite evident that you had never read in any form of literature what the duties of a ruler were. Having garnished the votes of the people your shamelessness remained intact since you offered nothing in return but a life of hardship and drudgery.

"None of the potential you spoke of could be achieved without the efforts of the Guyanese people but you broke their spirits and the probable remained potential. You cannot blame the prices of sugar, bauxite, rice, and imported oil for your

---

[g] *The Teaching of Buddha*, 95th ed., 1984, p258.

failures. They were common to all countries that were in trade. Yet none of those countries endured what Guyana had to bear – perpetual drudgery. I have pointed out to you how imprisoned the people are and their only salvation lies in greater production of the products they produce and the diversifications they can make. Of course the market forces will determine the outcome. Presently there is the air of freedom and ugly fear has taken flight. What a wonderful feeling to feel free, to be able to be critical and to know that victimisation will not take place. Allow me to recall for you what the Secretary of State for the Colonies, Mr Oliver Lyttleton, said in Britain's House of Commons on 22nd October, 1953, in his defence on suspending the constitution,

What emerges from British Guiana is a coherent picture of ministers largely dominated by communist ideas, who are... threatening the order of the colony, threatening the livelihood of its inhabitants and undermining not only its present economic stability but also chances of building it up... they are unfortunately all part of the deadly design to turn British Guiana into a totalitarian state dominated by communist ideas.[1]

"When I think of what has happened to Guyana I can only say that the statement made by the Honourable gentleman was indeed prophetic under your administration and he made that statement so long ago. You accomplished all he spoke of all by yourself and while in total control. According to him what you did was based on communism and not cooperative Socialism.

"Your departure from the Upperworld was so sudden and unexpected that I am sure you did not have time to leave a will for the people apart from the one for the family. I think your will for the people would have read something like this:

'I, Linden Forbes Sampson Burnham, O.E., S.C., President and Commander-in-Chief, also known as the Kabaka, Founder Leader and Moulder of Destiny, scholar and orator, a lineal descendant of Ananaias and the repository of sovereign power,

---

[1] p.xix

being of sound mind and memory (but of failing speech) do hereby devise and bequeath unto you my beloved people of Guyana the following, and I direct my legal personal representatives and trustees of my estate, powers and authority to ensure that my wishes are fulfilled:

(1)   A constitution which gives my successor immunity from all charges against impropriety, criminal and illegal acts of any sort, whether in office or not.

(2)   A financial debt which would be twenty-five times the debt which you carried when I assumed power and authority over you.

(3)   The commanding heights of the economy controlled by nationalised organisations run on the principles of party paramountcy and free of the burdens which competence and proper management require.

(4)   An electricity supply system that guarantees blackouts and continued damage to machinery and equipment.

(5)   An education system which will determine your academic and technological development by reducing its offerings and by making what is offered more appropriate to your economic and social conditions so that you will be unattracted to the ways of the modern Western industrialised world and its demands and be free of them.

(6)   A water supply system in Georgetown that would not have enough pressure and which water would have a coloured tinge to identify it with its source. For the remainder of the country I direct that the roadside taps and other systems of supply, which were in existence when I took power, be de-activated to relieve you of the

burden of having to maintain and replace them now or in future.

(7)   Health care institutions which cause you no financial burdens for expansion, replacement and maintenance of proper equipment and payment of adequate staff. My people do not need such institutions and I declare them free of those burdens which they will never be capable of bearing.

(8)   A system of roads, sea defences and drainage which will be and remain decrepit throughout the country.

(9)   Pensions determined by privilege that would ensure that your lives are as short as possible and which would provide you with passports to the world beyond to relieve your suffering and anxiety without unnecessary delay.

(10)   A system of taxation many times harsher and more oppressive than the Kaldor taxation, to which I objected in 1962 during my quest for power, and beyond what I proposed on 22nd December, 1968, in the hope that you will refrain from thinking of Western style development, which is unsuited to the condition I moulded for you.

(11)   A currency which will devalue from $1.70 G to 1 US dollar, which it was when I took power, to a depth lower than $125 G to 1 US dollar at which you will be persuaded to free yourselves from purchases overseas and the demands of Western manufacturers and producers of goods and services, these being unnecessary for your life when I am departed.

(12)   The virtue of self reliance and the beggar's syndrome, which will develop the ability to take from all charities in all conditions at all times.

(13) Two unsettled border issues which, if they go against you, will leave you smaller and poorer, which is in keeping with the destiny I was moulding for you.

(14) The continued influx of mosquitoes which cause malaria.

(15) The banned list of items which includes flour, split peas, cooking oil, magazines, newsprint etc. etc..

(16) Burnham Standard Time which will allow you to wake up earlier and to go to bed later since darkness will come much later.

(17) An electoral machinery with mechanisms that ensure that the PNC stays in government thus assuring the paramountcy of the party over the people, the army and the police, and maintaining corruption, nepotism, incompetence and inefficiency.

(18) I direct that my commands be adhered to and respected so that the SMALL MAN will have the opportunity to become a REAL MAN no matter how great the demise of the economy or the rise in levels of freedom from work or the opportunity to have work.

(19) Kuru Kuru College for development and re-orientation so that you may eliminate from your minds Western ideas and values and be trained to attain your full personalities in the new environment I have so carefully moulded.

(20) I direct that your main institutions be continued on the basis of a racial democracy and spoils system and that you will continue to have a President with sovereign immunities in and out of office, a parliament which will meet as little as possible and be a rubber stamp for the

President's wishes, together with an executive which will be under no proper judicial control.

(21) I leave you a truncated judiciary and declining standards of public justice with judges and lawyers and students beset by falling standards and I direct that standards shall be continuously reduced from time to time until you are free from the shackles of Western legal institutions, and for the merits of Palm Tree Justice, which I hereby declare to be and leave as a commodity which shall be subject to dealings as all other commodities on the open market all – for your absolute use and benefit.

(22) I leave you the Police State to guarantee and enforce the virtue of obedience to the laws and subservience to the system of justice which I have moulded for you.

(23) I free you of the need to protect or preserve life, liberty or property in any manner which is not embraced in the institutions I have moulded for you.

(24) To those of you who, being reactionary, wish to embrace Western values, Western learning, Western arts and Western culture, who love the economy of a free market and who already leave the country at seventeen thousand per year, I grant the freedom to emigrate legally or illegally whether or not your families are split into many parts in distant places all over the globe.

(25) I have declared, determined and moulded your destiny for the foreseeable future and I leave you the assurance that I made it certain that my successors in office will not be able or willing to alter or vary what I have left you.

(26) To each of those who will lead you and exercise power and authority over you after I am departed I bequeath a

granite cross, as a symbol of their strength in carrying the responsibility of ensuring that you enjoy the benefits of the inheritance and destiny which I have bequeathed to you as the declared objects of my bounty.

(27)   Lastly, I leave to you the speeches in my book, *A Destiny to Mould,* which, having been written, serves as a guide to all political aspirants to show how through honey-coated oratory, confidence can be won and promises made without a duty to perform.'

"I am sure there were many more bequeaths that could be made but it would be labouring the point! This was not an easy will to prepare but I trust that it contained most of your wishes. I am not a lawyer but I have tried to do it as you would and I do not think the contents will be contested.

"I will have to go shortly but before I leave I want you to make every effort to appear in a dream to someone dear to you beseeching that person to get your symbolic body removed from the Botanical Gardens. Heed my words! I want you to do this so that the people of Guyana will get another chance at being successful in becoming a prosperous nation.   Unlike creatures of the sea and those that fly in the Upperworld you need a passport or visa to move from one sector to another in Hades kingdom and that passport can only be granted if your body is removed. The curse that is cast by your body residing among the living is real and it truly hampers the progress of the country. Your legacy is bad enough and it will take some doing to change the will I mentioned. Every living Guyanese will have to be involved in order to change that. When your body is moved that of the other person will soon follow. I am sorry that my visit is short but there is not much one can do in under three hours. However, it may have been much more uncomfortable for you had I stayed longer as there are so many passages in your book of speeches that contradict your actions. Not mentioned in your book is your spy network but I would have liked to touch on that subject. Your network started from among those who worked for you at The Residence and spread to every nook and cranny of all government offices and state-owned enterprises. Your messengers followed your instructions without query and you were fed information about everyone and everything. You probably learnt that technique from Hitler's Gestapo.

"I must be fair to you, and express my sincere thanks for your insistence in getting those speeches compiled in a book. But you have tarnished them through your actions and behaviour. They also have become counterfeit since there is no relationship between the spoken words and the deeds performed. Can it ever be said that you were a man who stood for and upheld Democracy? Did you make the small man a REAL MAN? Was Guyana left with abundance and prosperity? Was Guyana left with a small financial debt? Could the health care and education systems left protect and bolster the Guyanese people? Is there a tale that is worthy that could be told? To those questions and many more the answers are all negative. However, without the speeches I would have been at a loss and I can categorically say this book that I am writing would not have been possible. You would have escaped published criticism and as the years go by your book would have remained the only evidence of your past and those reading it would have been misguided. I have titled my book *A Mouldy Destiny – Visiting Guyana's Forbes Burnham*. You must admit that it is appropriate after Guyana's experience, your performance, your legacy and my visit to you here. You did yourself in by having those speeches published. If I were a practising lawyer I would imitate you and say, *I am putting it to you that you did not act in accordance with the words you spoke. You did not practice what you preached.* It was not your fault. It was Destiny obeying Fate! The time needed to spend with you to discuss all the errors you made requires many more hours. I have not mentioned anything about our youth, and theirs must be a rough existence beginning with their lack of suitable food during their infant years. Their education must have suffered not only from an academic point of view but also morally and culturally. Recall what you said on 19th May, 1968, when you made a statement to the nation on the occasion of National Youth Week, ...*Theirs is a world to build for their parents, themselves, their children and their children's children so that this and succeeding generations may enjoy full and happy lives in this magnificent land of ours.*[1] They are hardly in a position to build anything for anybody, including themselves. The environment in which they grew up was one of deceit and their exposure to seeing evil practices on a daily basis have placed them at a great disadvantage. The development of our youth is so important since they are the ones who will be the inheritors and they must be properly trained and educated to take over.

"We have two major racial groups in our society and they cannot exist without each other. They need each other. In many ways they are complementary. Generally they live in harmony, and have done so ever since I have been aware of them. It is only when the political power game is being played that the rhythm ceases. As I see it (and you will agree although you may say differently to suit your ends), there will always be ethnic support on both sides. Therefore, to really achieve success there has to be an accommodation and in my view a coalition until someone comes along who would gain the respect and admiration of both races. Ideologies have no place to play in a society like ours. I have told you before that the population is too small, and the country is too rich. Everybody can have a good life that other peoples of the world would envy. Every Guyanese wants to advance. They all want jobs, housing, education, health care protection, recreational facilities, places to worship, good roads, adequate transportation, social security, a strong and honest police force and many other things which are taken for granted in other

---

[1] p.215

countries. They want all of the things mentioned in a clean and safe environment. They want to see their children grow up and become model citizens making a contribution to the society. Now, when you think of Guyana with its human and natural resources, what I have mentioned is easily achievable and there is no need for animosity and distrust. Guyana is not going to disappear nor will it melt away. This is a country which does not experience hurricanes nor earthquakes nor volcanic eruptions. Many of its citizens will live fairly long lives if treated properly, but how long is that? Seventy, eighty years, or a little more or less? It really does not matter provided they are content and happy. Think of how long you will be down here and that is when time really matters. Several generations will pass through Guyana and you will still be in this sector and the time will only begin to get shorter when your body is removed.

"And what is all the fuss about ideologies. My ideology is – bread on the table, jobs for the people, adequate housing, good health, good education, good friends, freedom of worship, good sports and nothing bitter, although that is inescapable sometimes. How beautiful it is to see the sun rise in the morning and to watch those beautiful sunsets in a free and happy environment! Both events created and directed by the hand of God. No mortal can bring about that!

"And what about the things that Guyana has to offer? Must it not be shared? I believe that Guyana must be a testing ground because it is such a lovely place with nice people and many good resources. And how do you pass the test? Very simple, you live with each other and you help each other to achieve the good things in life. I know Guyana has good things to offer because I have tasted of it. Many people will share my view but you have made things bitter and the youth of Guyana who have been exposed to your mould do not know how sweet it was – as sweet as ripe sapodilla[h] or yellow-skinned papaya.

---

[h] Very sweet and fleshy fruit, *Achras Zapota*

Banjoboy, when I think of those beautiful fruits we have, and of those fishes like lukanani, hassa, butterfish, bangamary, red and grey snappers, gilbacker, patwa and fine shrimps, and an occasional labba (did I see you smile when I mentioned this?), and those beautiful and varied dishes that are prepared, Guyana is really heavenly! It must be close to lunch when I start to speak this way and I really should get back upstairs. Before I go I must tell you that roti, dhollpourri, channa, sweetbread and many other flour products are back, like in old times. Butterflies are returning too! Boy, if you saw those red delicious apples! And they are available all year round now. I must say that most other food products that you banned are back in circulation and with them the smiling faces are returning, although it is not easy because of the value of the dollar. It really is a steep drop, like when water falls from the top of Kaieteur. In a kind of way you are still winning because if people cannot readily afford to buy as they would like to do then it is a partial victory for you. Maybe when your symbolic body changes residence from the Botanical Gardens the situation will improve faster and then all will be back to normal. In the Upperworld you achieved your lifelong ambition of political power and domination but having reached that pinnacle you brought misery and pain to a gentle people. You have left them with Herculean tasks as you betrayed them, but for a little more than thirty pieces of silver. Here in Hades you have been granted a taste of the experiences of those upstairs. You have probably gathered by now that I like to express myself in verse and it would come as no surprise that I have recorded you this way. I am going to read you my poem, 'Forbes Burnham', and as I read it I want you to indicate by some action if anything I say is not in keeping with the truth. I know that if you fidget too much then the barbed wire will come into play. My own view is that there should be no need for you to fidget. I must tell you that it is fairly long as it was not easy to cover your adventures in a short version. Relax and listen as it is all about you.

Forbes Burnham was Guyana's first Executive President.
Absolute power was by far his worst achievement.
As a youth he was bright and very clever too,
Winning from QC the Guyana Scholarship of 1942.
In 1945 to London University by ship he travelled,
Delayed until the Second World War was settled.
At London University he studied with other scholars,
Graduating with the degree of LL B with Honours.
He was recognised as a very outstanding speaker.
From Gray's Inn in 1948 he qualified as a barrister.
Returning, he established himself in the legal fore
But law was not enough as he wanted so much more.
It was said that in England he was a student of Marxism,
But his speeches courted dubious cooperative socialism.
Politics he entered with Marxist dentist Cheddi,
Together they founded the still existing PPP.
Leadership wrangling forced a split eventually.
Forbes Burnham later was the founder of the rival PNC
Which I later called the People's National Catastrophe!
But other opinions in the course of time
Said the anagram stood more for Poverty, Nakedness, Crime!
The two personalities need not their politics have shown
For soon each leader had loyal followers of his very own.
Like marriage vows in a ceremony that are put asunder,
Power intervened to claim the heart of a single partner.
This cleavage now placed the country in serious jeopardy,
Clouding Guyana's hopes for peace, progress, prosperity.
The electoral system which the British had in place
Gave Jagan's PPP a better chance to win the race.
Burnham called for changes in the system of election,
Confident that Cheddi will ultimately lose selection.
To the UN he said, 'No one party will ever be the champion,'
Thus there must take place a political accommodation.
Anti-communist America pressed Britain, to changes accede,

Replacement proportional representation did indeed succeed.
Burnham came to power in December nineteen sixty-four,
The victorious PPP out of Government as evident before.
D'Aguiar's United Force joined Burnham in a Coalition,
Quickly Burnham worked on parliamentary seat manipulation.
The unhappy marriage was annulled in nineteen sixty-seven,
Fragile Democracy went in search of a much safer haven.
Burnham, through electoral fraud and contrived rigging,
Sent the opposition parties to the world complaining.
There was no use in protesting about the certain cheat,
A-C America wanted Jagan's PPP out of the driver's seat.
Guyana got its independence in May of nineteen sixty-six,
Unprepared for the advent of Burnham's diabolical tricks.
A brilliant orator with flawless words of glorious promise
Which were betrayed like when Judas planted his famous kiss.
Burnham became a harsh dictator and very authoritarian,
Army, police, people's militia, Rabbi suppressed a nation.
Undated letters his appointed ministers were forced to sign,
Surfacing whenever he wanted them from government to resign.
He banned items such as oil, split peas, wheaten flour,
No longer did the people have bread, and roti to devour.
He banned so much, including harmless, cherished joy,
It forced me to give him the nickname 'Banjoboy'.
The Guyana dollar was also banned to isolation
Since it could not be exchanged outside the nation.
No more was foreign currency in general circulation,
A slow 'death' now descended and engulfed the nation.
He severed connections with Britain's Privy Council
To strengthen his hold and further flex his muscle.
The last fortress of justice and hope was out of reach,
Nothing in the Republic could hold nor stop the breach.
And now to be like Olympian Jupiter did he aspire,
Encouraged by unchallenged fraudulently acquired power.

The 1966 constitution removed and replaced so soon
With one that made the President absolutely immune.
The godlike status did not his signature change, I think,
Like always, assents continued to be penned in purple ink.
As Democracy and Justice fled the helpless nation,
Guyanese were also bent on quick and serious emigration.
They fled to many countries, near, far and wide,
From harassment, oppression and tyranny to hide.
Scholars, skilled workers, talented, disheartened Guyanese
Could no longer grin and bear the cruel Burnham squeeze.
The scattered families now found joy replaced with pain,
No more in one place would they gather ever to remain.
New burdensome taxes were passed and imposed hurriedly,
The afflicted Kaldor budget seemed palatable as curry.
The country's economy went tumbling fast and very far,
It seemed no different from a vanquished falling star.
Thrown into chaos by failing nationalised organizations
Guyanese were now deprived of much greater expectations.
The education and health care systems now failed to deliver
What Guyanese hoped would be their pride and treasure.
Financial debt to border Mount Roraima's height accrued
As falling production of bauxite, sugar and rice ensued.
Burnham dined, wined and chatted with leaders in the fore,
Mao, Wilson, Thatcher, Trudeau, Castro and many, many
more.
'Tis unknown if in silence they despised or called him 'heel',
The camera's many fruits do not these sentiments reveal.
In shiny jodhpurs on his horse he like a peacock strode
At Hope Estate, near Belfield, along the East Coast Road.
Like an overseer of a never to be forgotten bitter past,
On workers' overtime another ambition achieved at last.
Such acts confirm my view that he did not for people care
Yet he left a granite statue of Cuffy for all to stare.
Cuffy stands at Brickdam's head poised, ready for the run,
Burnham saw the need before the IMF audited the wayward
fun.

A brilliant and courageous son tried hard to combat evil
But in his prime was blasted by instructions from a devil.
It seemed as if Hope had abandoned this degraded nation.
On 6 August '85 Burnham went to the PHG for a minor
operation,
Sleeping, helpless, the Grim Reaper now silently descended,
A reign of terror unexpectedly stopped, definitely ended.
Sent to Hades' fiery halls to pain endure and suffer,
Guyana was now finally rid of the villainous dictator.
He had misruled just short of twenty-one years, you see,
As master of fraud, fear, chicanery and cruel tyranny.
The era was like when a sickness grips and holds on strong,
Penetrating, hurting, draining, visiting much too long.
The lifeless body decayed with every passing hour,
Caused by frequent cuts in scarce electrical power.
To be preserved like Lenin was the ultimate intent.
To Russia the rotting carcass on a Tupelov was sent
Where skills and chemicals would make it permanent.
But nothing could be done based on the rotten scent.
Some folks said that in life he was a very hurtful daddy
But on his return from Russia he became a helpless mummy.
A mausoleum with symbol in the Botanical Gardens reveal
The Russian counterfeit which makes Burnham look so real.
Now thousands who had suffered hurtful pain and sorrow
Prayed daily that another Burnham never again will follow.
Still a grip has he on the beleaguered territory
For his body does not abide in a lawful cemetery.
But until the symbol is removed to a lawful place
Poor Guyana will not progress and prosperity embrace.
Remove it henceforth and also his companion too
Then all good things will surely follow through.
Let those who keep baccoo[i] and practise legalised obeah
Confirm these portents are not the words of Cassandra.

---

[i] Similar to a genie in a bottle.

"I noticed that you did not even flinch once and that makes me feel so good. I was not very surprised as I knew there was no need for you to fidget. I must go now because I am hearing a familiar sound. My last words to you are, 'Remember the dream and make the best of the anniversary tomorrow'."

As I heard the sound of the hymn being sung I started to back away from the disembodied phantom keeping my body straight as I pulled back. I do not know if it was my imagination or if I actually heard but it sounded like,

Back to back, belly to belly.
Ah don't give a damn,
Ah done dead already.

It must have been my imagination since he could not speak!

I had not stepped back far when I saw the apparition becoming surrounded by an orange-reddish cloud. Then there was a sudden gust of wind, as if a storm was about to brew, and I saw one of the ballot boxes, which was on the ground, take flight and slam into one of the legs of the stool, causing it to tilt and hit the ground. Justice had been served although I could not see the apparition. Into view came many shadows and some looked familiar to me from my knowledge of world history. I had mentioned some already. This was really the abode of evil men. Men who had caused so many innocent human beings to suffer because of their desire for power. They were not visible to me when I was entering the forechamber but now I was being shown their faces as a reminder. My present knowledge told me that there were others still living upstairs who would join this unhappy band.

The phantoms receded and I found myself looking at different scenery which was becoming clear and I started to see vegetation and bodies of water, trees, palms, flowers, birds, beautiful butterflies and numerous animals. Some of the flowers I saw included bougainvillaea, golden showers, hibiscus, flowers of the flamboyant trees, various colours of flowers of the frangipani trees and sunflowers. There were so many that I could not name them all. It reminded me of scenes of Guyana. Amid them all I saw phantoms dancing and playing and I could hear faint music. These must have been the shadows of the good. There appeared in the background a rainbow with its seven splendid colours. It was so beautiful and peaceful there. I was being shown the place where people who do good on Earth eventually find themselves. I came to the conclusion that the Elysian Fields for departed souls of Guyanese was a place which resembled the country in which they lived and called home and it would probably be the place where they were happiest whilst on Earth. I thought to myself that if I did not adhere to the truth and honest speculation during my visit that I would never ever enter this forum, for although my subject was dead I did speak to him frankly and accused him of gross misconduct. If he is innocent of what I have said and written then I have sealed my own fate and in the future this scene will be just a memory or even erased.

As my thoughts meandered through the future I heard the voice once more. "Traveller! Your journey is ended here in the Underworld. You have joined a select number of people who have been given that chance. I trust your visit was worth your while and that your mind is now at ease. You have seen the punishment that is dispensed to those who have acted beyond their bounds and who have brought harsh treatment upon themselves. Only truth and justice are respected here and they provide an invisible shield from enduring such punishment. Wickedness and evil will always be severely punished."

The voice was now coming from before me as I continued my steps backward. I could barely see the face as the voice continued, "You are not an appointed messenger but let me share with you some thoughts. The life given to each person in the abode above is a gift and it is given in earnest. All are born free and share the same circumstances of birth. There are a few exceptions but that is only practised to ensure the safe receipt of the gift of life. You are aware that some lives are very short and return back to the Underworld. Others live for a long time before returning. Despite the circumstances which exist, no individual is given power over another. Those individuals who find themselves over others must remember that it is a privilege that has been granted them. In political life those who have been chosen to serve others must realise that it is a privilege and should not be abused. The privileges granted are given in the name of the people and thus those individuals who are fortunate to be chosen become the servants of the people. Those granted life are not given that life to harm others. Life is a gift and must be cherished. No one must do to another what one would not do to one's self. The gift of life although measured by Time is also monitored by deeds and it is those phenomena which determine the final resting place. Being king, president, prime minister or whatever, does not give the power over life except in those instances which contravene the law of the land. Those positions I mentioned are privileged and holders must remember that their privileges are only temporary. The pathway of life is strewn with temptations of evil, hanging like berries on a vine, with the fat and succulent berries representing the most awful acts of evil such as greed, covetousness, desire and ignorance. Those who eat those attractive berries cannot escape the murky realm of Hades."

The face of the voice was becoming clearer and I thought I recognised it. It was a face that I had known throughout my life. I longed for the face to come much closer but it kept its distance. This was the face of my queen of mothers. This was the face of a lady whose devotion to husband and children was unparalleled. I was about to speak when the voice continued, "What are the benefits of war? None. War is horrible and results in loss of precious lives, destruction of property and waste of scarce resources. It brings sadness, ghastly atrocities, misery and hurt. The only beneficiary is the ruler of Hades since his domain increases in numbers. All mankind are brothers despite the hue of skin. Discern not by colour but from what lies within. Judge on disclosed character. All have red blood running through their veins and although they may worship differently they all belong to the human race. It is important to remember this and only mankind has been granted the power over other living creatures. Examine life and it will be seen that its necessities are simple.

"Is friendship so difficult to achieve? Is diversity of culture such an obstacle? Is offering the hand of kindness such a chore? Mankind must build on friendship as it is a bond which can be infinite yet strong and with boundless reach. Friendship beckons mutual understanding. It prospers with assistance to one another. Friendship, kindness and love are the jewels of the Earth. Their cultivation will lead to untold satisfaction. Conflict, hate, distrust and jealousy are the enemies of man. They must be shunned. Remember that Time, always regarded as the great healer of wounds, is also the measurer of life and travels continuously, never stopping for a breath. Time harvests the years, leaving only memories, faint or strong. There are sectors here other than the Elysian Fields which are becoming overcrowded because of mankind's folly. Many wreak havoc on helpless people stealing from them the little joys that they encounter. Many accumulate fortunes at the expense of others, desecrating the values that have stood for years. Many are so greedy and speak lies cloaked with appearances of sincerity. They think not of retribution which is inescapable. Truth and honesty are hidden and seldom surface in their lives. They never worry about those who endure pain and suffering and who on many nights are hungry and without solace. So much is done that is unworthy of mankind who seems forgetful that the power to bring about change is totally in his control.

"I caution you to remember the words of the man from Galilee, *Love one another, as I have loved you.* I must leave you now with love and kind regards to all the folks."

I shouted hurriedly, "Mommy, wait!" But the voice and image vanished. When she spoke of friendship I remembered a picture which hung on the wall of our home in Charlotte Street and these words were printed there,

The chain of friendship stretching far
Links days that were with days that are.

Before I could ponder further I heard an earthly voice saying, "We will now sing the school song." My voice blended in with the audience singing:

Laude qratemur scholae
Nostrae conditores:
Disce, nam iubent, ludo
Et labore mores.
Corpus sic tibi sanum
Sana mens servabit.
Reginae Collegium
Sic honor ditabit.

Scire nos monet vitam
Disciplina patrum:
Splendide mori docent
Nos exempla fratrum.
Lux dei discentium
Corda illuminato!
Reginae Collegium
Ista laus ornato!

The ceremony was now over and, as I turned to hail someone, a friend came up to me and asked how I liked the proceedings. I told him it was very nice and I thoroughly enjoyed myself and was very glad that I had come for the reunion. He then said, "Jim, did you notice that no one mentioned Burnham's name during these celebrations and tomorrow is the anniversary of his death? No one said anything at all about him, and to think of what he has done to the school and to Guyana! It was as if everybody wanted to forget that he ever existed or were afraid to say anything. What do you think?" I replied, "Boy, you may not have heard, but somebody did say something."

Glossary

Bangamary – A Salt-Water Fish Similar To Whiting

Bara – A Pancake-Type Bread Made With Split Peas And Flour

Black Pudding – A Sausage Made Of Rice, Seasonings And Blood

Butterfish – A Salt-Water Fish

Butterflap – A Type Of Bread Roll Made With Butter

Channa – Another Name For Chick Peas

Coconut Biscuit – A Biscuit Made With Flour, Sugar And Coconut Milk *Collar* – A Bread Cake With Coconut Flakes

Dholl – A Seasoned Broth Made With Split Peas

Dhollpouri – A Pancake Made With Flour And Crushed Split Peas

Duff – A Bread That Is Cooked With Steam

Frangipani – A Shrub With Widespread Branches Bearing Flowers

Genip – A Fruit Similar To Lychee And May Be Related

Gilbacker – A Sea-Water Catfish That Could Be Very Big

Hassa – A Freshwater Fish With Tough Scales

Jumbie – Similar To A Ghost

Labba – A Vegetarian Eater Of The Rodent Family

LBW – Abbreviation For 'Leg Before Wicket'

Mauby – A Beverage Made From The Mauby Bark

Metemgee – A Dish Made With Ground Provisions, Coconut Milk, Plantains, And Containing Fish, Duff And Boiled Eggs

Nuttin – Candy Made With Peanuts

Obeah – A Type Of Witchcraft Similar To Voodoo

Patwa – A Freshwater Fish Related To Tilapia

Pepperpot – A Dish Made Of Meat And Pork, Real Demerara Sugar And Containing An Extract From The Cassava Plant

Pine Tart – A Pastry Containing Crushed Pineapple

Potato Ball – An Appetiser Made With Seasoned Crushed Potato

Roti – A Pancake-Type Bread Made Best With Ghee

Shirtjack – A Stylish Shirt Worn Outside The Trousers

Souse – A Dish Made With Pork, Containing Lime And Lemon Juice, Onions, Pepper And Cucumber

Sweet Bread – A Bread Containing Sugar And Raisins

Tennis-Roll – Bread Kneaded In A Special Way With Very Fine Texture And Containing Sugar

White-Eye – A Small, Sweet Cake

References

Burnham, Forbes, *A Destiny to Mould*, Longman Caribbean Limited, 1970

Bukkyo Dendo Kyokai, *The Teaching Of Buddha*, 1984

Bullfinch, Thomas, *Myths of Greece and Rome,* Penguin Books, 1981

Clarke, Laurence, *Queen's College of Guyana – Records of a Tradition of Excellence,* published by the author, 1994

Chronicle of the 20th Century, published by Jacques Legrand, 1989

Dickens, Charles, *A Christmas Carol*, Penguin Books, 1987

Virgil, Publius V., *The Aeneid*, Penguin Books, 1990

The Constitution of the Cooperative Republic of Guyana, 1980

Yansen, C.A., *Random Remarks on Creolese*, published by Sonja Jansen, 1993

Appendix One

THE QUEEN'S COLLEGE SCHOOL SONG
(*Carmen Collegii Reginae*)
(Latin Version)

MUSIC COMPOSED BY HIS EXCELLENCY
SIR WILFRED COLET, KCMG
WORDS BY HIS EXCELLENCY THE
HONOURABLE C. CLEMENTI, CMG

I

Laude gratemur scholae
Nostrae conditores:
Disce, nam iubent, ludo
Et labore mores.
Corpus sic tibi sanum
Sana mens servabit.
Reginae Collegium
sic honor ditabit.

II

Divae nos Victoriae
In fide vivamus:
Nutricem Britanniam
Rite diligamus!
Sic nos patriae virtus
Discentes fovebit:
Reginae Colllegium
Sic du florebit

III

Scire nos monet vitam
Disciplina patrum:
Splendide mori docent
Nos exempla fratrum.
Lux Dei discentium
Corda illuminato!
Reginae Collegium
Ista laus ornato!

C. Clementi

Appendix Two

THE QUEEN'S COLLEGE SCHOOL SONG
(*Carmen Collegii Reginae*)
(English Version)

ENGLISH VERSION BY MR ALLEYNE LEECHMAN

I

Praise and thank we godly men
Who, at our Foundation,
Did decree that work and play
Should be our salvation;
Strive must we with hand and brain
Ne'er the twain dissever-
Wooing Wisdom cheerily-
QUEEN'S, QUEEN'S, FOR
EVER!

II

Sacred text and hold theme
(Jesu! To Thy glory!)
Ancient lore and names of might,
Wealth of word and story,
Great deeds shared from age to
age,
Courage failing never.
Link us, Britain, long to thee-
QUEEN'S, QUEEN'S, FOR
EVER!

III

Ruthless war on blood-soaked fields
Claimed, afar, our brothers;
Shrieking shell and creeping cloud
Saw them die for others:
Ours the guerdon and the crown
Of their high endeavour-
Dead, they held our lives in fee-
QUEEN'S, QUEEN'S, FOR EVER!

Alleyne Leechman